Dedication

To Taragon, my first dragon.

Look for these titles by
Emily Veinglory

Now Available:

King of Dragons, King of Men

Coming Soon:

The Kin Series:
Wolfkin (Book 1)

Father of Dragons

Emily Veinglory

A Samhain Publishing, Ltd. publication.

Samhain Publishing, Ltd.
577 Mulberry Street, Suite 1520
Macon, GA 31201
www.samhainpublishing.com

Editing by Anne Scott
Cover by Anne Cain

First Samhain Publishing, Ltd. electronic publication: August 2007
First Samhain Publishing, Ltd. print publication: June 2008

Chapter One

The heel of Xeras's boot flapped loosely as he walked through the gloom of the forest at dusk. At first he had limped on in hope of finding a village or a forester's house, somewhere to beg for a night's shelter and a scrap of food. But the road had become more erratic and faded into a haphazard path. Finally, as he stumbled over a tree root, Xeras realized he had lost his way altogether. There was nothing to see all around but steep hillsides, bereft of any tracks but those made by the hooves of wild animals. He stood, listening to the subtle sounds of the trees, leaves whispering in the wind. Xeras was so weary he could barely focus his eyes and so hungry the world hardly seemed real. Perhaps it would all end here, curled up cold and alone in the dark forest. He found that he didn't care.

Between the branches he glimpsed a curl of pale smoke barely visible against the indigo sky. The Gods alone knew what the cause could be here, so far into the hills.

But you are curious, darkling. It was always your problem, eh? Why don't you go see?

"Be quiet, Drin," Xeras muttered. "Can't even death save me from your nagging? Well, not your death apparently...maybe mine will do it."

Go have a wee look, my dear. Could be some nice little farm, a huntsman's camp or a woodman's shack. You can always lie down later, you know. The afterlife isn't going anywhere.

Xeras felt as if his knees were about to buckle beneath him. The quiet sounds of the trees faded into a roar like a distant waterfall. And through it all he could hear Drin's warm, sourceless voice so clearly...

You know I'm just going to keep nagging until you do it, darkling. When could you ever deny me anything?

"Aye, well, there's that." Xeras took a deep breath and took a few steps further, holding his hands out to fend off the scratching branches. One step, one more, just one more. He walked out of the undergrowth into a small clearing where the grasses crackled underfoot. Before him, the hillside was split by a rocky chasm. Pale vapors wended from its mouth and the darkness within the great cavern stirred.

A flickering glint floated towards him like an errant firefly. Xeras watched with muted fascination and only gradually came to understand. The tiny light was the reflection of the moon in the eye of an enormous creature whose head extended towards him. From the tip of its snout to the crown of its sloping brow, the creature's head was a little longer than the length of Xeras's whole body.

The dragon blinked.

"Well, here's a good cure for curiosity, I should think," Xeras said to nobody in particular.

The dragon stared at him and he stared right back, calmly awaiting his demise, feeling a slight smile crease his face, even.

Say hello to the lady, my dear. And back away, slowly.

It was, perhaps, fortunate that Xeras's occult education included some basic words in the tongue of dragons. Well, the education required study of a language and choosing the

10

ostensibly dead tongue of the apocryphal dragon race had been his own idea. If he couldn't make his father proud of him, he could at least make him most abjectly and absolutely disappointed, even in his achievements. Not that such juvenile preoccupations mattered now.

"Hello, ma'am. Or is that miss?" he ventured.

Dragons were a sigil of Tirrin, but scholars had long debated their actual existence. If the myths were in any way accurate, very few people got to see a dragon before they died. Even fewer, he imagined, got to see one and live. It didn't bother him. In fact he could honestly say: "You are so beautiful."

Moonlight only hinted at her verdant scales as she reached out for him, folding her armored digits around his chest and lifting him effortlessly. The last few stitches of his flapping boot heel surrendered and it dropped into the mud as Xeras closed his eyes and prepared, with some equanimity, to meet his fate.

ℂℨ

Said fate did not seem to be in a hurry to arrive. Instead, Xeras found himself borne, with a slightly uneven, three-legged stride, into the utter darkness of the cave. The dragon's claws encircled his chest just tightly enough to make breathing difficult. The air inside the cave was warm but stale, and dry, adding to a feeling of suffocation. There was a scent, like sweet spices burning and tilled soil—the black dirt of the mountain turned for the first time in spring.

Xeras, you can't sleep now.

Drin sounded alarmed. Xeras felt himself lowered onto a surface that was hard and warm at the same time; made up of what felt like different lengths of tree trunks and branches. As they moved slightly, sliding beneath him, he realized this was the coiled body and limbs of the dragon, cradling him gently like a bowl woven from stout branches. The dragon's infinitely flexible length made and remade a shallow bed that perfectly supported his weary body. Gently employed talons inspected him with some interest. Xeras's limbs ached as the chill leeched out of them and he stretched, luxuriously lying in the restless juncture of her sinuous limbs as easily as in a hammock.

The skin of the great beast was so smooth it eased past him pulling at his ragged clothes. He felt tired, half-drunk and floating. Even wide-eyed he saw nothing in the inky blackness of the cave, not even his hand in front of his eyes. He laughed, feeling the sound well up from inside. Was it possible to be drunk on darkness?

His jacket tore, with the muted crackle of broken stitches, and pulled away from his body. The scent grew stronger now, sweet like a field of flowers being crushed under the feet of a marching army. His body almost seemed to melt away until he was just an errant spark of awareness, a moon-mote floating in a dragon's eye.

His shirt had been little more than frayed strips of cloth fastened by the vestiges of collar and cuffs. It drifted from his body and his skin kissed the skin of the dragon, sparking into sudden sensation, smooth and hot, to the smell of quenching steel and thunderclouds onward rolling. His trews and boots released him, delivering him up naked into the writhing embrace of scaled skin. Nothing could hurt him here, for it was surely a dream...

Xeras lingered in twilight; he heard Drin's voice calling out to him but the words drowned in a dark ebbing tide and the crackling sound of fire. For the first time that ghostly voice was dimmed and pulled beyond easy reach of his consciousness. Xeras rolled gently, and a long wet tongue ran up along his thigh, brushing past his groin and rasping across his chest. He stretched, languorously indifferent to the strangeness of his embrace. He hardened, and yielding flesh pressed against his belly, rubbing. He could feel the bruised petals falling from the sky and settling on his flank and side as he arched in release.

Cʒ

Time flowed by, slow as cold syrup.

Xeras...Xeras.

Xeras moaned and tried to block out the sound, raising his hands clumsily. Grit beneath his body coated a surface of uneven rock. Loose pebbles ground beneath his fingers as he turned on his side. Sensations fell in veils, stale smoke and faint light flickering through the dust thick in the air. The open expanse of the cave dropped away in front of the broad ledge he lay upon. The air tepid and fading towards cool...a nagging itch in his side made his skin twitch. Reaching down, he felt a great insect bite on his side.

I don't think you should wait for her to come back, lover boy.

A very different voice answered Drin. Low and booming, but human enough that Xeras looked around expecting to see a man standing in the shadows, but no one was there.

"She won't be coming back."

Xeras shivered. More voices, just what he needed. A formation of rocks in the centre of the cave...he did not recall it being there before, but he hadn't really been cataloging the cave's features and furnishings at the time. The outcropping crumpled and moved, resolving into a great shape, almost lost in the gloom but for its crested spine. Another dragon, larger...a male perhaps. Hopefully not one given to jealousy. Xeras's memories of the previous night were thin and gaped with tears and holes. At least this dragon spoke a human tongue; it was hard to imagine it considered humans merely as prey.

"But that was not last night," the dragon said. "Some time has passed. Plegura left you almost immediately, females are often like that. So I stepped in to ensure the opportunity was not lost."

The giant form of the dragon arose from the ground. With each movement its form became easier to discern. In appearance almost exactly like stone, limbs looking like rough-hewn rock beneath folds and shards of armor, great spines and thick neck with loose skin that hung in ragged, pocked folds. Great wide jaws dominated the dragon's broad head, with tiny eyes barely discernable except when it blinked. Its entire form was rough and foursquare, in stark contrast to the female's sinuous curves.

"Opportunity?"

"Oh yes. There are so few of us left and situations amenable to breeding are infrequent. Come with me, child. I will explain as much as I may. It is quite the task that has been set before you."

With heavy steps the behemoth lumbered away through a giant gash in the rock that led outside. Xeras curled his legs and pushed himself up. His outstretched arms looked thinner even than he remembered, and with a tickle, his hair fell forward, down almost as far as his elbow. But he felt...better, actually—quite strong. He clambered slowly down to the even dirt of the cave floor, not seeing the remnants of his clothing anywhere. Dim light beckoned from across the cavern.

You might as well see what the dragon has to say.

"Ah yes, Drin. Of course, because following your advice has worked well for me so far."

Not that his own influence on Drin's life could be called...constructive, on the whole. And besides, there was just one obvious way out and little point in cowering naked in the darkness like a rat in its hole. Xeras's feet felt strangely soft as he walked tentatively through the debris of the cave and along a rift that gradually showed daylight overhead and then spilt out of the hill into a meadow.

The bright sunlight revealed swaying grasses speckled with seed heads and surrounded on all sides by leafless trees. It was as if the lingering summer had died overnight into early winter. His first thought was that the field was broken by a great outcropping of stone about the size of a two-storey house. Then the dragon swung its head towards him, blinking its tiny black eyes blearily and he saw he had been fooled again.

"Every dragon is different," it said. "Plegura is a swift flier; her flaming breath charred this whole valley. She is, as you remarked, most beautiful—but not, it must be said, much of a conversationalist. We are shaped by each of our parents..." The dragon seemed to muse on that a while. Falling into its most unlifelike stillness as if it truly were more stone than flesh.

Xeras waited, feeling terrified and foolish in equal measure as he stood there grimy, naked and listening to the discourse of a dragon—albeit a dragon that seemed to be most amiable and wise and not currently inclined to consider humans a finger food. Xeras scratched his side where the bite continued to itch.

The dragon's wide brow crumbled into a massive frown. "I really wish you wouldn't do that."

Xeras froze. "Do, ah, what?"

"Just stand still while I explain... Now where was I? Ah, our parents, the parent of a new dragon get, I mean. They consist of the dragon female, the dragon male and the human. And how exactly the human became involved in the process is a long,

long tale. One I hope to eventually tell you, for I believe it would be of interest to you. But for now, it is enough to know that you *are* the father of a dragon."

A shiver of shock and revulsion ran through him. "This Ple—whatsit. She's pregnant?"

"No, dear boy. You are."

Xeras's hand smoothed over the irritation at his side. Glancing down, he saw the bite was a small lump, very much like a bee sting or a small abscess, but distinctly green in color and iridescent in hue. The hollow of his stomach lurched. He wanted it off, out. Gods, the last thing he needed was to be infected by some monstrous thing. And he didn't even want to think about how it would come out...

The dragon continued to watch him, blinking those little black marbles of eyes. "Unlike Plegura, I was raised by a gentle, scholarly woman," it said. "We, none of us, get to choose our parents. But with dragons particularly, they do after a fashion get to choose us. My human mother taught me a love of reading and the arts—she left me with a lasting urge to be sociable. There are, around the edge of the forest, a number of people I meet with to discuss the works of philosophers, the uses of medicinal plants, and many other matters. I did take your clothes to a very clever young woman who lives near the village of March, but she declared them quite beyond use and secured you some replacements. They are, I understand, of a poorer quality of cloth and not much decorated, but newer and apt to wear better."

The dragon's gaze indicated a parcel wrapped in leather that nestled amongst the dying grasses at the mouth of the cave. Xeras looked at the package and back at the dragon. Dammit, but there was little point in beating around the bush. He indicated the inflamed lump.

"Will it kill me, this thing?"

"Oh, quite the converse. Dragons are often slow in growing and their influence, both before and after the separation, is to significantly extend the human parent's life. And more importantly, the circumstances that allow us to reproduce require that a human come to us, one of the right stock, who is—how should I put this?—in want of reason to live. That requirement has distressing effects on our infant mortality rates, but it is meant to ensure the matter is more of a boon than an imposition for the man or woman involved. I hope, I most dearly hope, that giving life to one of our so scarce and dwindling race might provide that for you."

I always wanted children.

Xeras clapped his hands to his ears and squeezed his eyes shut. His knees collided with the ground and he bent forward into the grass. This craziness changed nothing, this perversion that took on Drin's aspect and muttered inanely to him day and night, giving voice to his own insanity. If his ears could lie to him, why not his eyes? Maybe he wasn't in the forest at all. Maybe he was still back on Tirrin in his small white bedchamber and only his mind had walked out onto the solitary road.

He crouched, feeling his breath heave through his body and bile, sour in his mouth—waiting for something, anything. But all that happened was the itch in his side grew more intense. He reached up, his fingers clawed over the spot, but stopped. He looked up into the broad face of the dragon now standing before him.

"So what am I meant to do?"

"You go on with your life," the dragon said. "You do what seems right. We have found that to give any clearer guidance is rarely advisable. The character of a dragon and the way it is properly succored, these are both best simply allowed to emerge, naturally."

Xeras wasn't going to say it, but "natural" was not the first word he would use to describe his situation. The stone dragon turned from him and put one great paw on the scarred surface of the rock. Xeras flinched, expecting the clash of stone on stone, but dragon and mountain seemed to seal together without a sound.

"But you'll help me?" he pleaded. "You can tell me something, anything?"

"Sadly, I have already told you all I can. But do not worry. If you only try, you will raise a fine dragon son...or daughter. And find it a situation not without benefits for you and your kin."

The dragon reared up and placed its other fore...paw—hand? It was somewhat intermediate between the two—on the rock and in great shaking steps began to ascend the sheer slope.

"A daughter, I hope," it mused. "No more than one in ten of us are female, and many of them, well, peculiar sorts. It will be the end of us...soon. We have waited almost too long to find a new conduit, a new continuity."

Slowly but inexorably the dragon scaled the rocky slope until its heavy tail lifted off the ground with a surprisingly dainty flick. At each step, the dragon melded seamlessly with the stone beneath its feet.

"You can't leave me," Xeras said plaintively.

You said the same thing to me, darkling. But saying cannot make it so. Let the creature go. Dragons don't have a reputation for being good for a man's health.

The dragon said nothing further as it climbed gradually out of sight up the steep mountainside. Xeras threw pleas and curses after it until he could see it no more. He stood panting, itching and frustrated, scuffing his feet on the ground.

Now that you have gotten that out of your system. Why not look in the parcel?

"Shut up, shut up! Gods damn you, Drin. You're dead. You're dead because you had to have me and no Gods-damned law was going to stop you. Because you couldn't keep your fool mouth shut and so were discovered. I watched you die, Drin. You're gone. If you want to punish me, what more could be done than this?"

I loved you.

"*Loved*! Loved? And you don't now? What, the dead don't love?"

Would you prefer I moan and weep and haunt you like a vengeful spook? Why would I do that? I knew the penalties for miscegenation—for affairs between a noble and mere peasant like me. And you're right; it was my own gossiping that doomed me. Now go look in the parcel, Xeras. There's nothing much to be gained by throwing a tantrum at a dragon, especially as he isn't here anymore.

In anything other than affairs of the heart, Drin had always been the sensible one. Xeras sighed, threw his hands into the air...and bent down to open the package. Tightly sealed within were tunic and hose, a cloak and belt and upon the belt a small purse with a handful of battered coins, a rough hand-drawn map marked with an emphatic dotted line with its terminal "X" showing the way to the nearest town, and even a hunk of slightly moldy tack-bread. At the centre of the bundle was a pair of boots, not new but with wear in them. Everything but the undyed leather boots was, like his old clothing, black. The dragon's friend had been considerate—but then perhaps such charity was to be expected for a new...mother. Hardly a father if he was going to bear the damn thing and presumably raise it.

No. He'd find a town and use these funds to get himself a knife. Dragons be damned. Only so much that could be asked of any man. He dressed and walked away from the cursed cave with vigor and determination, seeking the road he had been upon before straying into the woods. Wading through the grasses towards the tree line he pushed back memories... Drin laughing in the darkness of their hidden meeting place, talking as they lay together sated and complete. Drin had wanted children. But then Drin had wanted Xeras, Drin had wanted to be a blacksmith...Drin had wanted to live. Drin, living or dead, would just have to forgive Xeras one more thing, and that was all there was to it.

Chapter Two

It began to rain. And from the way it fell, this was clearly the sort of smug, persistent deluge that meant to be at it for days. Xeras pursed his lips and forged on through the whipping saplings that sprang back at him with every step until he broke into the dark void beneath the canopy of the larger trees. Instead of providing shelter, the trees just seemed to pool the water up and drop it in cupfuls that hit his head and shoulders like well-aimed, wet slaps.

He could hear Drin, a constant presence, humming in the back of his head, but Xeras was determined to pay him no more heed. That phantasm, madness or whatever it was, had caused him enough heartache already. Drin was dead, and by now surely buried, time to leave him be. Xeras kept the image in mind of a nice keen dagger and a private place to deal with what that misbegotten she-dragon had done to him. He tried not to even think how the dragon *father* had become part of the process. It a blessing that he didn't remember.

The water made his hair hang down in sodden, ropelike strands. Just yesterday it had been cropped close to his head. Now it fell almost to his elbow. Dragon magic or unmarked time? No matter, just another use for the dagger when he got it, and no need to think any further than that.

His side itched sullenly and he rubbed it through the coarse cloth of his tunic with the flat of his hand, oddly reluctant to hurt the thing until the deed was done. No need to be cruel, after all. Finally he found the muddy channel of the roadway, two wheel ruts divided by a band of sodden, broken-down weeds. He hopped awkwardly over the mud to walk down the outside edge of the left-hand track. Hunching over to shield the rain from his purse, he removed and unfolded the map. He traced one finger down the rough sketch line of the road and past a crossroad. At the end a cross marked in a small, neat hand as "Ballot's Keep". As far as an immediate goal went, that would have to do. He had to hope the person who made the map, and so suggested the destination, possessed some notion of good sense—probably more than Xeras's own meager allotment anyway.

I would hardly s—

"Shh."

For once that actually worked. Maybe it was a bit like with dogs, they only really listen when you're angry enough to kill them if they don't. Which would be a little redundant in this case.

Of course he had no idea of the distance; the map was not marked with any kind of scale. The weather glowered with stormy promise, but he was already wet through. There was no reason to delay. As Xeras walked, his anger stayed with him. He worked his way up a steady slope for hours, until the sky grew dark, his empty stomach clenched up like a fist, his heels blistered and burst, and every sinew of his legs screamed for mercy he wasn't inclined to give. Fool, fool, fool, he cursed himself. Somehow finding a way to make even the most dire of situations worse. Lost, alone, haunted, an exile and now infested with a dragon get! What next, a plague, a curse, a pack of sadistic wolves armed with flensing knives?

The rain kept falling but he didn't care. He couldn't get any wetter. When it grew too dark to see, he crouched by the side of the road under the dubious shelter of an ant-infested, overhanging cliff, gnawed at bread in a state well past stale and slept fitfully until dawn when he began his journey again with a dull determination. His mind was so fogged he barely remembered why he was walking, or where to, but an evil temper festered beneath his exhaustion, waiting for a focus.

Intermittently his mind wafted back to the horror that had sent him on this ill-fated journey. They hadn't just killed Drin for his temerity—they'd tortured him, too. They would call it the time-honored penalty, handed down from Tirrin's greater days as an empire that stretched all the way to the edge of the high barren plains. They had walled Drin up within a dungeon with all the water he could drink and not a morsel to eat until he was a curled-up travesty of a man and finally died. The bloodline of Tirrin that ran through Xeras's body must be kept pure, they declared, and any who sullied a person of that line were meant to suffer before they died.

No matter that two men could hardly produce a mongrel child. No matter that Xeras had railed and begged and beat his hands bloody, that he had refused food until they forced it into him with a tube. Tears formed in his eyes, but Xeras blinked them away as he marched on. It had been a slow kindling love; an affair started more by Drin's amiable insistence than any fast flaring passion. But by the end he'd loved that man with every fiber of his body and the entirety of his soul. And maybe that's what he'd lost, his soul, that such things now happened to him. Maybe a life of privilege had made him soft, as Drin always said.

I said it tenderly and I meant it fondly.

Striding down the road as swiftly as his stiff legs would carry him, Xeras beat back emotions he could not tame. Well, look where the laws of Tirrin had gotten them. He'd like to see the Tirrin elders take the matter of the bloodline's precious purity up with Plegura, oh Gods he would. Not that he was best pleased with her himself.

A distant sound broke through his reverie. Xeras scratched his side, then stopped. The infuriating itch came and went. He pushed his hair back from his face and the rain made it drop down again. What did it matter if he scratched the little beast? After all, he meant to cut the damn thing off first chance that he got. An unexpected sound thrust through his preoccupations. A muted clatter from somewhere behind him made him turn. Xeras could see nothing, the road bent around and his view was cut off as it curled and cut down the side of a wooded hill.

He stood and peered up the road as if it held an answer. A small carriage approached. It was drawn by two large, plodding tawny horses that pulled stoically at their broad collars and didn't seem to mind the incline much. It drew up to him. A driver huddled beneath his cloak, reins in gloved hands. He pulled the horses up short and they braced themselves obligingly to hold the carriage in place. One horse reached out its pallid muzzle towards Xeras's face and snorted curiously, blowing up a fog of breath.

"Get out the way, won'tcha." The driver had a round, impassive face not marked by any particular expression, but as Xeras stared at him, he shrank back in his seat. Xeras, well, he just wasn't in the mood to be cooperative. In fact he was in a mood to become very uncooperative indeed and this was the first real chance he had to express it.

"No," he said tersely. "I won't."

Manners, darkling, Drin chastised, making his presence felt again and apparently not put off by Xeras's lack of response.

Xeras ground his heels into sodden earth, ignoring the comment with all his will and feeling as stubborn as an overburdened mule.

A young, bearded man appeared from the side of the carriage, holding the door open and leaning upon it. "Is there a problem, Prem?"

The driver turned to him, rather mournfully. "This gentleman here is blocking the roadway."

The young man peered at Xeras with a slight squint, suggesting that his eyesight was less than keen. "Is there a problem?"

"Well," Xeras explained with exaggerated care, "that rather depends on how you look at it. I am going to Ballot's Keep, and you are going in that same direction. I am going on foot, which is not only a damp and exhausting proposition, but also rather slow. You are traveling a little quicker and in a lot more comfort in this sound carriage of yours. Now as it happens I am on the road ahead of you. So I could get courteously out of your way and let you travel on—no doubt splashing me with mud in passing—or I could walk, even more slowly, all the rest of the way knowing that those well-mannered horses of yours are not likely to run me down."

"Or," the young man added, "as we are all going to Ballot's Keep we could do the sensible thing and offer you a ride."

"What?"

Drin's laughter tickled his ears. *I like this one. He'll drive you crazy, my dear.*

The young man smiled slightly at Xeras's surprise. "Was that not what you were, in your own rather interesting way, suggesting?" His open, wide and rather pleasingly symmetrical face seemed just as charming as his words. His eyes were rather small, which was an unwelcome reminder of the stone dragon, but as he was in possession of a carriage Xeras was willing to forgive that one small failing.

Xeras stood and stared at him for a moment. The boiling edge of his anger refused to dissipate even in the face of what certainly seemed to be good will. As he walked to the side of the carriage, they could simply drive off and leave him behind, but that suspicion was forestalled as the man jumped out onto the muddy verge and gestured for Xeras to climb in ahead of him.

With really no sensible objection to make, Xeras walked over and peered into the dark interior. Two bench seats faced each other. On the forward-facing seat sat a young woman in a demure but densely embroidered grey dress who regarded him with amusement. "Why don't you get in before you get soaked?"

"It is a little late for that."

But Xeras did clamber in and sat with a distinct squelch on the rear-facing seat. The young man jumped back in spryly and seated himself next to the woman. He pulled the door shut again with a vigorous jerk, and fastened it. Xeras stared at them both incredulously, incensed that in their charitable good sense they gave him no obstacle to rail against, nothing to fight. Sure, it was an irrational feeling, but with an infant dragon passing for a boil on his stomach and the ghost of his dead love whispering in his ear, Xeras didn't feel inclined to be rational.

"I am Katinka," the young lady said with a nod. "This is my brother Carly—the Ballot Duke."

"The Ballot Duke?"

"You don't know what that is?"

"No and please don't explain. I imagine you get tired of doing it and I don't really give a damn, so I might as well save you the trouble."

Carly laughed explosively, slapping his hand on his knee. A knee that Xeras noted, reflexively, was attached to a substantial and well-muscled thigh. The man's overall frame was rather impressive, if built more square than lithe. Xeras glared at him, even finding the man attractive angered him.

"Here's one who might give you a run for your money, Tinka. And he has prettier eyes than you to boot."

Prettier all 'round, but we won't hold that against her, Drin piped up. But Xeras was determined not to react to his asides any more, let alone when others might see it.

"I can hardly help that I was not born with bright green eyes," Katinka replied primly. "And I really don't care what you seem to be suggesting about my character or that of our guest. Some of the old boys at the keep may think me a harridan, but I don't see them complaining when doing as I ask gets the drain working properly or stops the food from spoiling."

"I don't have green eyes," Xeras interrupted.

"But you do," Carly corrected with a bemused glance. "Bright green eyes, as my sister was kind enough to mention. And not an unpleasing shade at that."

Xeras looked at him, then leaned his head back against the seat as the carriage began to rumble down the road. He'd liked his eyes hazel; Drin had liked them that way too. "Damn it. That really is taking a liberty."

If he ever caught up with Plegura, dragon or not, they were going to have *words*.

CR

The awkward silence must have lapsed rather quickly into sleep that consumed the greater part of the day. Xeras came to groggily, with his head hanging to the side and thumping periodically against the paneling of the carriage. He didn't rush to make any move. On the whole he'd rather be asleep again, but he could hear Carly and Katinka talking.

"He's thinner than anyone should be allowed to get, Carly," Katinka said.

"So you're going to keep him? This isn't a one-eyed kitten or a colt with four white feet. You can't just keep everything that follows you home."

"You're only saying that so you can pretend it's all my idea when Chamberlain Parlen has a look at him and gets all on his hind legs about taking in vagrants. After all, you're the one who invited him in, and I can see the way you're not looking at him."

"I'm what? Sister dear, that doesn't make a bit of sense."

"Oh come now, Carly. When you take a liking to a man, you won't look directly at him. Did you think you were being subtle or opaque? You have many fine qualities, Carly, but that is not one of them. I sometimes think I know who you fancy before you do."

"Nonsense," Carly said with the resigned tone of a man who knows he isn't fooling anyone. "I'm not some callow boy to go mooning after strangers."

The carriage shuddered. An enormous jolt propelled Xeras forward. His eyes flew open and he threw out his hands to catch himself. He found his fingers clutching Carly's padded tunic and looking up into his warm brown eyes. It was a hard gaze to meet because it kindled something inside Xeras that he would rather leave cold. Turning aside, he found the panel pulled down to show the view outside. The rain had stopped falling and the warm buttery light of late afternoon was glinting off the rain-polished rocks and foliage. Of course, once he had actually found shelter it *would* stop raining.

He could not see the road at all. The land dropped away so sharply from the side of the carriage that it displayed only a sweeping view of a town nestled on one side of a small basin, surrounded by forested hills and snow-capped mountains. The buildings were thickly built of dark wood and pale grey stone, and a great structure like a bridge blocked the far side of the valley. Behind it all, mountain ranges towered like jagged teeth. It was so different, so far from the slender, pallid towers of Tirrin, not only in the miles he'd traveled but in every rough-hewn detail. Sure, he had fled his home island and everything it represented, but the foreign shapes of the crowded roofs were still strange and unwelcoming.

Give it a chance, Xeras. Winter's coming and you've gone about as far as you can before spring.

Xeras pursed his lips and looked out over the cliff. "If you're planning on driving us off a mountain, you could have the decency to not wake me up for the experience." Xeras peered over the ragged edge just a few spans beyond the wagon's wheel.

A glimmer of movement, out of scale, suddenly brought it home. The slight fog of smoke rising was not from chimneys of the houses. That sinuous movement between the steeply canted roofs was *her.*

Carly said something about his faith in the driver and said driver's vast experience with the route. The usual platitudes, Xeras hardly heard him.

Xeras sat back in his seat. "Plegura."

"What?"

Katinka raised her hand to silence her brother.

"We must get down there quickly. There is a dragon in the town."

ᏣᏍ

The carriage seemed set to shake itself apart as the big horses hit a thunderous canter, storming down the steep slope into the town. Xeras braced his arms and feet, pushing himself back. Trees and buildings flashed by and the smell of smoke grew stronger until the carriage finally shuddered to a halt.

Carly pushed the door open and leapt out. He called up to the driver, "Get them out of here."

It was all very impressive as Carly drew the short dagger from his belt and strode heroically towards the dragon. But Xeras didn't have time for the niceties of traditional hero-dragon interactions. Nor any particular desire to see Carly squashed liked a bug.

He jumped out of the carriage just as it pulled away with Katinka protesting inside. Plegura had a horse carcass hanging from her jaws as she reared, casually sideswiping a two-storey building that started to crumble inwards. She towered up, higher than the buildings, her scales sparkling like a jeweled mosaic and her eyes deep black shadows that hinted at secrets no man was meant to know. The sight of her, in fact, caused some very unsettling feelings. Simple, uncompromising anger presented a more palatable approach.

Xeras, I really do not recommend...

Xeras's longer stride allowed him to overtake the duke.

"Dragon!" Xeras shouted in the she-demon's own tongue. "Damn you!"

All his fear, disgust and discomfort crystallized into simple rage. Dragons just weren't enough to scare him anymore.

"Hey, don't..." Carly called out.

Plegura's mouth gaped and the dead horse fell to the cobbled street with a wet splat. Xeras advanced, bending to pick up a splinted length of wood. Plegura's swanlike neck drew up and she shuffled one step back.

"Plegura, damn you, what the hell did you do to my eyes?"

He swung his makeshift weapon, threatening to beat her armored hide with a piece of timber that had already demonstrated itself somewhat less than dragon-resistant.

Before he got anywhere near her, Plegura turned her whole body in a graceful arc and retreated down the road. Her long tail gave one last whack to the trembling house so that its great street-facing wall bulged and trembled outwards with an ominous groan.

Xeras sprinted after her, but nothing could match the speed of a fleeing dragon. She unfurled her wings and leapt into the air. Xeras could only hurl his makeshift weapon at the arrowhead-shaped spur on the end of her tapering tail before she was borne aloft by great beats of her wings. Dust and debris spun into the air. Xeras was buffeted from his feet and slammed into the ground as the draft pummeled him. He struggled on his back, a position that provided only one benefit: a good view of the damaged house as it collapsed with a roar on top of him.

Chapter Three

Dust choked his lungs as his ears hummed with the aftershock. He didn't want to move. It felt as if nothing could really be wrong so long as he didn't move. Xeras lay, now on his front, in the shocked stillness of having the better part of a building descend from on high, realizing with some surprise that he was still alive. Something pressed across his back, pushing down but not hard.

The building fell on you, darkling.

Xeras pressed his forehead down onto the dirt. Gods-damn but it was impossible to ignore a man's voice, even if it couldn't possibly be real. "I know that, Drin," he muttered. "How could I conceivably have failed to notice that? And please, please stop using that pet name. I never did like it."

Drin just laughed. *Wiggle forward a bit. It's a bit tight here and your rescuers jumping around on top might get you killed yet.*

"My what?"

But he could hear it now, shuffles, creaks and muffled voices from overhead. There was not enough room to get up on hands and knees, and too dark to see anything but a few glints of dust hanging in the air. He pulled himself forward with his arms, slithering his body side to side to get free.

"Darkling," he muttered. "Darkling, what the hell does that mean, anyway?"

Except that Drin had been his light. A self-aware and serious child, Xeras knew he had grown into a dour and scholarly young man used to the privileges of his rank but doing little to earn them, still living in his father's house. He had many associates but no particular friends and as he moved through the tipping point of manhood and found the first grey strands in his black hair, he stumbled into love. It was not falling, certainly. It had begun with the new houseman and his insolent teasing whenever they were alone.

"Sure I'll get those trunks brought in for you, master Xeras, but only if you smile for me. Just once so I can see what it would look like..."

A thick post was jammed into the ground ahead of him and the whole structure of the rubble trembled as something above him cracked loudly. There was a sound of timbers settling and others creaking with strain.

Keep going a little farther. Do it for me. I'm not ready for you to join me quite yet.

It meant nothing, an echo of a dead man through an addled mind. Yet somehow the strength and will came up from within him. He could see light ahead and, squirming onto his side, he eased around the obstruction. Pushing off with his feet, he grasped the rough edge of a fallen chimney stone and heaved himself out into the open air.

"There he is," a voice called out.

Blinking into the light, Xeras tottered down, stepping across a series of precarious footholds to the ground where a crowd at least three or four people deep welled up to meet him. Hands grasped him and pulled him bodily down into their midst. The duke, Carly, was there. He looked strangely elated to see Xeras alive, given that their waking acquaintanceship could not be counted in units larger than moments.

With a final anticlimactic quiver, the rubble behind him slumped and settled all but flat to the ground. A rather portly man pushed his way through the crowd and bustled past the duke to grasp Xeras's forearm with a damp, proprietary manner. "Well, your Lordship," the man said apparently to Carly. "You have actually done something useful in Pitrick town. That was where you found him, I assume. Come with me."

Xeras had not realized that the last barked comment was directed at him until he was jerked almost off his feet. The crowd broke in general cheering as he was dragged up the street; many reached out to clasp his hand or clap him upon the back with an enthusiasm that bordered upon assault.

Such a cheerful, well-dressed and physically powerful people these townsfolk of Ballot's Keep. Somewhere in the increasingly confusing blur that his life was becoming, he noticed that, other than the bits that had been discourteous enough to fall on him, it seemed like a nice place after all.

CB

Near the head of the main street, at the foot of the great structure that, close up, did not seem to be quite the right shape for a bridge, stood a tall house made of grey stone and thick beams of wood aged to the color of peat. Inside he found himself ushered into a receiving chamber where a great fire blazed and the air had a quality Xeras had almost forgotten the feeling of...warmth.

The presumptuous gentleman deposited Xeras in a great padded chair. "You will be staying, of course." It wasn't really a question, not even a rhetorical one.

Carly and Katinka straggled in afterward, conversing together in low whispers.

"Well it's nice to be wanted," Xeras snapped as he rubbed his belatedly released arm and tried to ignore the other aches and pains of his body. "But I think you'll find I go where I please."

"See," Carly observed to his sister. "Just like one of your cats." Xeras glared, but found that Carly did not seem to notice the disapproval as he stepped over to a large sideboard and idly poured liquor into a stone goblet. "Chamberlain Parlen, along with a good portion of the citizenship of this small town were rather impressed at the sight of a large dragon fleeing from you in obvious terror. That particular dragon has been decimating our livestock, driving out crofters to destitution and knocking down buildings all over the place in the process."

He passed Xeras the cup. "So long as you can keep it out of Ballot's Keep, we could make it worth your while."

Parlen huffed. "Did you see it run from him? Of course he can keep the dragons away and of course he will be staying." He fixed Xeras with his beady eyes, as if to suggest that the mere hint of resistance would be very unwise indeed.

Xeras looked back holding his expression neutral, he hoped, and wondered why the rightful duke of this teacup duchy seemed to live in fear of a man who resembled the product of an unfortunate pairing between a sow and a badger. He took a deep drink from his cup, a fortified wine of some sort and terribly sweet. He could not suppress a grimace at what passed for fine liquor in these parts.

"Could you keep it from returning?" Katinka asked pragmatically. She showed all the signs of being the only sensible person in the room.

"Her," Xeras corrected.

"What?"

"The dragon, Plegura, is a female. And it is probably safe to assume she will not be coming back into town so long as I am resident. The females are sometimes *like that*, I am told." Katinka looked as if she wanted to ask "like what" but she refrained. "As for keeping away all dragons," Xeras confessed. "Under the circumstances, I can't really guarantee that. Not in the long term."

"Well," Carly said. "It is only the big green one who has been storming through town in the last few years. So I guess it would be worth a stipend, something reasonable, to keep her away. You could, ah..." he added with studied casualness. "Stay here. There are some suites free at the back of the house. It's a little dark but..."

"Well, it should suit me fine then." Xeras stood abruptly, without giving his head enough notice. The room dimmed and seemed to rotate about him. Apparently if one refrained from eating properly long enough even a sip of wine was more than sufficient.

"I am sure that..." Katinka paused to place a solicitous and subtly supportive hand under his elbow. "Your name is?"

"Xeras."

"Seras?"

"Close enough."

"I am sure you would like a chance to bathe and get some rest. We can discuss any other expectations in the morning."

CB

Xeras settled into a tub made from waxed wooden staves

and filled to the brim with water almost hot enough to scald. It had been set up in the room they were bestowing on him by two young but altogether sturdy maidservants. As they installed and filled it, they stared at Xeras like he was the most fascinating thing they'd seen since the last two-headed calf.

Once he was left alone Xeras closed the door, stripped off his sodden clothes and lowered himself in. A single sound of satisfaction escaped his lips, somewhere between a grunt and a moan. He scrubbed his skin and lathered his hair. He rubbed off every bit of grit and grime and a good part of his skin to boot. He wrung out his hair till it squeaked and let it fall back from his head, over the edge of the bath until it brushed the floor.

Tirrin men kept their hair short and artfully styled. Xeras's fine, straight hair had always resisted the preferred style of rows of curls like a coiffed sheep. Perhaps he would leave it as it was. At least it could be tied back at this length. And it might be one small gesture he could make for Drin, who had kept his hair like a peasant was meant to, long and plaited up. But in bed at night, it had lain in a mass of riotous curls, ruddy highlights catching the candlelight.

Carly stepped through the door. "Hey."

"I don't require a bath attendant, let alone one with a big gold chain around his neck. Doesn't that chafe, by the way?"

You're not fooling anyone, my dear.

It seemed to be difficult to get a rise out of this man. Even for a northerner, he was square of shoulder with a broad, bland face not built to show emotion. Carly had an apparent immunity to rude remarks.

Perfect for you in at least one obvious way, then.

Needless to say, Carly came into the room with blithe assurance, certain of his welcome. Xeras slid down modestly but the low height of the tub didn't help him much as his knees bent and poked up ridiculously in response. Given that covering more than one thing with his hand would be less than subtle, he opted to cover the dragon bump. Now that was telling.

Carly closed the door behind him with a smile. "I'll get your back." He watched Xeras rather closely but given the size of the room, he was still a good five strides away.

"I have long arms; I can reach it for myself."

The door opened again to admit an older woman bearing a bundle of cloth. She stepped inside with the smooth efficiency of household staff. It was getting a little crowded in a room he'd been given to understand was his own.

"I knew this was too good to be true," Xeras muttered to himself.

Walking past them, the maidservant pulled out a wooden chair and drew it over to the foot of the tub. Over the back she folded a bath sheet and robe. She exited just as perfunctorily.

"No point being bashful now." Carly leaned against the wall beside the door. "Whatever you have or don't have will be well known all 'round the house by morning."

"Her?"

"Limry is 'she who knows'. One of the reasons she ended up in that role is that she makes sure she knows the sort of thing people want to know, but don't necessarily want to find out for themselves."

"Charming."

"I'm not one of those people."

Oh ho, a little subtlety behind that amiable face. Was Carly not curious or just not timid about it? Maybe the former as he mercifully stayed about as far away as he could without leaving the room. So he might be hard to offend, but at least he could take a hint. Xeras felt a twinge of something he didn't like. Minor nobility or not, Carly was a decent sort of person. Of course he could have warned Xeras about the nosy Limry. But Xeras didn't have anything to hide in that department anyway, at least not now that he'd warmed up a bit.

His thoughts continued to unspool even as Xeras found his eyes drifting closed. The next thing he knew he was choking and being dragged out of the tepid bathwater by his hair.

"I think you might be done," Carly said. "Parlen would not be pleased if I let our new dragon bane drown in a bath tub."

Carly leaned over the tub, his elbows dipped into the water, its surface covered in soap scum that might be thick enough to hide a thing or two. His face was scant inches away from Xeras's, the duke's breath puffing over his damp skin. For a moment he thought the man was going to kiss him. He could swear the desire was there in his eyes, but they were so close he could hardly focus properly to see. His head, feeling too heavy, fell back, Carly's fingers still tangled in his hair.

The whole world was reduced to the hand cradling his head and the square handsome face before him with a closely trimmed beard tapering down from his sideburns. It was a disappointment and a relief when, after a long awkward and silent moment, Carly released him.

Carly actually blushed as he passed over the bath sheet and Xeras reached for it, realizing that he had done nothing, absolutely nothing in response. That must be why the poor man was now acting rather confused. Did Xeras even have it in him anymore? Like hell, why would he throw himself off that particular precipice again? No, after a night's sleep he would...he would be able to decide what he was going to do about all this. It seemed like discomfort was the only thing keeping him awake. He wasn't going to be able to think clearly until he'd got his head down for an hour or two.

"I guess you can take it from here." Carly took his leave, offering what was probably meant to be a reassuring smile. "But I hope we have another chance to talk soon."

After he was gone, Xeras dragged himself from the tub and made a muted effort to get dry, snuffed the candles and crawled naked into the wide, waiting bed. He curled up with his back to the room and could hear Drin's voice singing some old lullaby so quiet it was barely more than a murmur. Xeras plunged into the first deep, dark real sleep he had known for months. And just as quickly into a bright, sharp and unmistakably prophetic dream.

Chapter Four

The wind shrieked around him like a river of ice. Even in the darkness beneath the rolling clouds, Xeras could tell they were high above the cover of the forest and the low hills. There was hard rock beneath his hands—and "we"? Yes, just ahead of him, Carly stood, braced against the onslaught of nature, staring out over his town. All around them, low mists and high clouds mixed in confused skeins. Expectancy filled the air as Carly turned to him and beckoned.

Xeras felt like a ghost in his own body, there but not there, and he knew what that meant. The whole point of the sanctity of the precious Tirrin blood was that it carried magic in many forms. But with each generation more and more Tirrin men were born "dull", no talents emerging from them. Xeras had thought himself to be in that number but he knew, deeply and innately, that this was a true dream. Foresight, rarest of the talents, had come to him late.

He looked around, frustrated at how few clues the tempestuous air gave him. When would this be and why was it shown to him? Carly reached out to him, shouting against the wind, but his voice was lost. What happened next sped ahead of comprehension. A great, armored hand snatched Carly. The hand of a dragon, pallid in color like the first petals of a yellow flower, bearing him swiftly away. Looking up, Xeras saw the beast's retreating form, sucked swiftly up into the stormy sky and speeding towards the coast.

Xeras just stood. His breath rasped in and out. The wind continued to howl, and Carly—was gone.

ᗅᔕ

"Seras?"

Xeras shot into awareness like he was falling from sky. He tried to get back in control of his limbs, hindered by blankets that seemed to have wound about him like amorous pythons. The squishy surface under his left hand turned out to be Carly's groin.

Don't stop there, darkling. He's not exactly pushing you away.

At which point the fickle blankets released their hold and slithered onto the floor, leaving Xeras to grapple instead with the ample charms of the desirable duke. He froze in place. Then rethought that strategy, snatching his hand back from the poor man's privates. Fortunately Carly was dressed in a starched and embroidered suit of clothing that rendered the accidental contact somewhat short of a serious insinuation. Less fortunately, Xeras had not bothered with bedclothes and removing his hand meant the rest of his body collapsed onto Carly whom he had somehow pulled onto the bed.

"I have...dreams, sometimes," Xeras offered by way of flustered excuse.

"So do I," Carly replied, quite unruffled. "Strangely enough they look a lot like this."

Xeras scrambled back, grabbing for the straying covers whilst trying to keep his arm casually draped across his little green parasite. "So we both wake with cock's crow, or cock at least. Is there some call for it?"

Carly laughed and rolled off the bed, landing on his feet like some big cat. There was something of that species in his expression also. "We had visitors from the illustrious neighboring Duchy of Thurst. They arrived last night and we are obliged to entertain them for the greater part of the day. They are an old dynasty with strange ways and a deep desire to marry one of their inbred daughters to the duke of this land. It is an offer made to many of my predecessors and none, to my knowledge, accepted it. The Thurstian nobles seem incapable of understanding that our ruling title is not, and will never be, hereditary. They are convinced their failure is because they have yet to offer us a girl pale enough, skinny enough or young enough...that being *their* taste in beauty."

Xeras managed to hold a corner of a blanket, the rest of which was caught on something under the bed, over a more or less random portion of his abdomen. He wasn't certain he had the right end of that insinuation and was too embarrassed to capitalize on it right now.

Carly wasn't helping either, looking Xeras up and down and covering his mouth with his hand, as if he realized that getting an eyeful of a man's groin and laughing was less than polite. "Just, um, feel free to wander around and get to know the place. Ask the staff any questions you might have. And they should be able to help you with anything you need, well most things." He indicated the table near the door. "I left you some funds and leave you to your own devices until we can speak properly tomorrow, or perhaps tonight if my diplomatic relations with the Thurstians run their usual precipitous course. Limry will bring you some breakfast. Or at least I am willing to bet it will be Limry. She'll be sorry she missed this..."

Carly backed out of the room and closed the door after

him—but muffled laughter could still be heard from the hallway. Xeras flopped back on the bed. He felt like he had hardly slept at all, but prophetic dreams were said to be trying. He considered spending the day in a second attempt at getting some real sleep and adjusting to the fact that he might have finally done something that would please his father.

He wasn't so sure that Carly didn't *deserve* to be abducted by a dragon. He certainly didn't know what he was meant to do about it. Sleep was banished now, anyway, and curiosity prickled along his spine. He had a new town, a peculiar prophecy and a quantity of coin. There were any number of things he could do...

But what would you want to buy with that coin that would be better than the toothsome duke, who was on offer quite for free?

"Like hell, that was just a nightmare-induced assault and he didn't strike me as very interested in pursuing it as a tryst. I'm amazed he didn't throw me out on the street."

For a bright boy, darkling, you can be very slow indeed.

"And for a dead man you do have a lot of opinions. Besides, you heard him. I hardly think a man who finds my body hilarious is ripe for seduction. I just hope to hell he didn't see this."

Xeras looked down. The dragon...thing was about the same size, but more clearly defined, like a glass marble. As he looked, a small shape moved within the taut boil like a tadpole still within the egg. Disgust welled up from his stomach. Hopefully the coin Carly had left him would stretch to something with a sharp edge. But his feelings about it had waned in intensity. He couldn't decide what was worse, that he was getting used to sharing his head with Drin's wraith or getting used to sharing his body with a monstrous fetus. Good sense and self-preservation indicated that both had to go.

C3

Despite Carly's predictions, a dour younger woman brought him food, enough for three men. He suspected that helping in the duke's residence was a hobby for a large number of women from the town, rather than a serious profession for a few. He intended to pay the meal little attention, used to his own habitual lack of appetite in the months since Drin's death. But almost without thinking, he reached out to pick up a round, unfamiliar fruit that proved to be tart and juicy. Shortly he had consumed more than he had in the last week—which was admittedly little more that most men would take each time they broke their night's fast.

Feeling unusually benign about the world, he donned his cloths, still damp and now somewhat crumpled, but otherwise in good order. Then he opened the shutters to discover he was on the ground floor, looking out into a crowded garden. He met the eyes of a dejected girl-child in a ridiculous party gown, sitting upon a bench seat. Her hair was beaded and braided, her face painted, and every inch of her ornately clothed, plucked, powdered or bejeweled. But the lines of her body drooped and crumpled into a posture of glum boredom. Xeras rather expected her to say something, but instead they continued to stare at each other for some time. Finally a liveried guard standing nearby piped up.

"Hey, you. Who are you? What is your function here?"

"I'm Xeras, and I deal the duke's dragon problems. I am sort of like a scarecrow, only a whole lot scarier."

"Very funny," the man snapped. "Now step away from the princess."

"Well, sir. The day has barely begun and I have already had my fill of being found amusing. And besides, I am within my own bedchamber. If the young lady finds my presence distressing then she will just have to step away from me."

That's telling him!

The girl's expression smoothed from a furrowed sulk to complete blankness, revealing a strange sort of prettiness and an expression suggestive of no great intelligence. The girl certainly was an interesting collection of features with enormous eyes, tiny chin and nose, long hair that was almost white and a slender neck like a dove—but the overall effect was more akin to a clever doll than a living girl.

"He's not bothering me," she said listlessly, kicking her feet from which peculiar shoes with high wooden heels dangled heavily. She slouched upright, positioning the ridiculous shoes under her, and walked over with a hesitant shuffling step and an audible rustle of starched skirts.

"Princess..." the guard admonished nervously.

She ignored him, and addressed Xeras. "My parents brought me here to marry me off to a stranger, but now they won't even let me meet him until *they* have finished talking to him. Don't you think that's the worst thing?"

Xeras rested his hands on the windowsill. "My parents disapproved of my lover so they had him tortured and killed."

It was very strange to just say it like that—as if it were no great thing. He felt Drin's constant presence inside him twist uneasily, as if he did not wish to be reminded of his demise, or perhaps his objection was to it being mentioned so glibly. The girl gave him a sharp, bird-like, jabbing look.

"Really?"

"Really. So why don't you stop sulking and find something to do while you wait. If you don't like Carly, you only have to tell him. His isn't one for crossbow weddings."

"I...who? For what?"

Xeras sighed, having no desire to unpack a throwaway comment for this human confection. "There must be something that you like doing more than staring into the bedchambers of strange men. I am sure the duke would want you to be entertained." Xeras cast a slightly apologetic look at the guard as he turned away.

"I like to ride," the girl blurted.

There was something almost desperate in her voice. With all the loose ends tickling around inside of him, Xeras truly wanted to ignore this dressed-up child and her problems, and sort out a few of his own.

"Are there horses here?" she added, speaking to his back.

Xeras turned back to her, lips pursed in annoyance. "I don't know. I just got here myself." He did not sound courteous, but she was lucky to get his cooperation. He wasn't going to feign joy. Still... "But as a couple of them accompanied me on the journey, I must presume they are still around here somewhere. I suppose we could find out," he conceded.

Xeras slung one leg over the windowsill and climbed out into the garden. He pulled the shutters loosely to and spoke to the guard. "You must have seen a stable upon arrival. Is it against orders to introduce the princess here to a horse or two?"

The big man wavered, deciding upon his response. Then he made a vestigial bow. "I am Durrin, sir. My role is to ensure the lady Phinia comes to no harm. It was her wish to walk in the gardens as she waited. I believe they proved less—extensive— than she might have hoped. The stable, I believe, is over here. Might one ask what sir's position is in the duke's household?"

Xeras took a deep, bracing breath and stretched his back,

feeling the stiffness in his spine from too many nights sleeping on the hard ground. "It is unfortunate you do not care for the answer I have already given to that question, for it would not improve upon repetition," he enunciated sharply, as he went in the direction Durrin indicated.

...and we need to have a few words about that, my boy. One encounter does not a dragon slayer make.

The duke's domicile was, it seemed, modest for his rank. Maybe the paucity of level ground in this mountainous region reduced the scale of the usual pretensions of nobility. It was still a great, sprawling house to be sure, but the garden and outbuildings were curtailed by high, bare rock cliffs that reached up towards the sky. To one side of the main building stood a large wooden structure, its front corner meeting the back of the house so only an archway the size of a normal door spanned the distance between the two. In front of the stable, there was a cinder-covered court where carriages could be drawn up.

The girl stumbled after him. She reached down and hitched up her layers of skirts and waddle-jogged to keep up with his longer stride.

"Phinia, what if your mother should see?" Durrin hissed.

Drin's voice seemed fainter than usual, *You actually like her, don't you?* Xeras just shook his head, exasperated. It hardly mattered how he felt about the girl, although why her parents treated her like a cross between trade goods and an enormous doll he did not know. But then his own father never saw Xeras as more than a source of reflected pride or shame, mostly the latter. If he had been born a girl, he might have had more in common with the princess than he cared to admit.

The stable was dark. Large front doors stood open to show stalls on each side.

"Let us see what we have. I have never sat on one of these creatures myself—nor do I see the appeal."

"You have never ridden a horse?" Phinia exclaimed with utter shock.

"I have my own legs." Xeras went to the first stall.

"These are our carriage horses," Durrin said. "And my master's hack."

The large stall held three mean-eyed, stick-legged creatures, two of dapple grey and one brown. Xeras had become used to the sight of horses after leaving his island home, but all four of these looked more like bastard sons of starved horses and dragonets, tall but thin and fiery. Their eyes flashed with near predatory interest and their nostrils flared as they snorted. Given what they had achieved in a daughter, it was not surprising to see what the Thurstian duke and duchess admired in a horse.

"You must try it," Phinia insisted. "I could teach you. I have an excellent seat."

I'm sure she does...

"My lady," Durrin interjected apologetically. "If your presentation suffers, the duchess will be displeased...with both of us."

Which suggested the princess was a nice enough person to consider a servant's fate. Not that it seemed her overriding concern. Phinia reached over and patted Durrin's arm. "And she'll make your life hell. Don't worry, Durrin, I would stay well out of the way. But really, can you credit it, a grown man who has never sat astride a horse? It hardly seems possible!"

"He need not concern himself with your appearance or my meager possibilities," Xeras said. "I am not going anywhere near one of *those*."

The Thurstian horses observed him in a way that suggested an even greater degree of disdain. But Phinia kept her skirts high off the ground and hobbled past him. In the next stall, there was a small fat pony whose function he could barely imagine—perhaps just a pet, as it had the ill-omened four white feet of the "colt" Carly had alluded to in the carriage. Then the duke's two stolid coach horses that looked over at them with mild interest. The rest of the stable proved to contain little more than discarded equipment and bales of straw and hay. She circled back to Carly's coach horses.

"One of them, then," she said firmly.

"I really..."

Phinia was already reaching for a bridle hanging with other tack from pegs on the wall. Durrin intercepted her grasp.

"If you will insist upon this, my lady. Go and stand to the side of the cinder court. I will assist the gentleman."

Phinia pouted, but conceded. "Bring the paler gelding out to the mounting block."

Xeras baulked. He had left a life of obedience behind and was not about to be ordered around by any passing princess with time on her hands. But...

Humor the girl. What does it cost you?

Chapter Five

The answer, apparently, was the last remnants of his dignity. The rather dusty riding saddle sat on the large horse like a tiny cap on an enormous flagon, with the girth strap let fully out. It took several attempts to get on the behemoth's back. Xeras's knee tended to give up and drop him down on the block before he could make it. Durrin had hovered like he was considering pushing Xeras's butt up onto the beast himself, a prospect that made seemed to make Durrin so nervous that, with one final, irritated heave, Xeras clambered aboard on his own. This left him straddling the broad, hairy back of the towering coach horse. It seemed even taller from up on top than it had from the ground.

"Take up the reins," Phinia called out.

Xeras grasped the thick leather strap uncertainly. He was quite pleased the horse seemed to be as ambulatory as a badly designed piece of furniture. It just sort of harrumphed and looked around at Durrin as if to ask what the idiot on its back thought he was doing.

"Grip with your knees," Phinia urged, "and take up the slack on the reins."

His sympathy for the sulky princess was fast evaporating as he contemplated the distance to the ground and the sheer size of this beast's hooves. The potential for various unfortunate conjunctions of the two with his own body came to mind. Nevertheless Xeras did his best to squeeze with his legs and pull in the reins. The horse huffed and tossed its head, snapping them right out of Xeras's hands. The leather loop sailed forward to dangle down to the ground.

Phinia let out a snort no prettier than the horse's and laughed. Xeras clenched his teeth together and tried not to look as terrified as he felt. Maybe it was an unfortunate alignment of the stars; today he was destined to be humiliated for the amusement of others.

Lighten up, kid.

"Lighten up, says the ghost of my dead lover," Xeras muttered.

It's just a horse. It won't kill you.

"Does *it* know that?"

Damn. So much for the plan of ignoring Drin.

Durrin stepped over and lifted the reins to him with a concerned glance. Xeras made a mental note—if he couldn't ignore the phantasm altogether, he did need to avoid speaking to him when anyone else might hear.

"Just dig your heels in, squeeze with your knees and move slowly forward," Phinia called out.

Xeras nudged the horse's sides tentatively with his feet. Its skin twitched like some fly was bothering it. Xeras tried again, more firmly, but to no greater effect.

"Do it like a man, for Gods' sake," Durrin hissed.

"I don't think this horse wants to go anywhere," Xeras observed.

"*You* are the one in charge," Phinia said.

"I don't really want to go anywhere either," Xeras added, quietly pleased the horse didn't seem to agree with her assessment.

Phinia started to laugh. Overhead, in the sidewall of the house, a large set of shutters creaked open. A portly, older man sporting a peculiar wig and a preposterously shaped moustache poked his head out.

"Phinia, is that you *laughing*?" he asked, as if the possibility was quite remote.

"Oh, I am sorry if I disturbed you, Papa," Phinia blurted. She looked upwards, her face flushing.

Xeras interjected, "Your daughter is of the opinion that every proper gentleman should know how to ride a horse. Perhaps I am not a proper man, or this is not a proper horse, but it seems this talent is not as ubiquitous as she suggests."

Xeras was acutely aware of his long, black-hosed legs hanging over the coach horse's great tawny sides like a spider astride an apple. He nudged the beast again but was rewarded with no response other than an extended almost musical escape of equine flatulence and a truly overpowering smell.

"Oh." The man leaned his arms upon the windowsill and peered downwards. He tried, with limited success, to hide his amusement behind his exuberant moustache. "Perhaps our man Durrin could try, ah, leading the horse."

"Oh really, Papa. You cannot expect a man charged with the extermination of dragons to allow himself to be lead around like an infant on a pony ride."

"My dear, you mistake me for a man with delusions of dignity," Xeras said flatly. It was a little chilling that she had translated his description of his dragon-scarecrow duties as something more like the lead role in a heroic epic, but he let that go. He peered around to get some notion of the horse's expression. Was it ill, tired or just taunting him? "I suggest we try your father's eminently practical approach."

A portly woman with powdered hair appeared beside the Thurstian duke. "Phinia, are you *actually* wearing that gown on a cinder court? You will ruin it, and your new slippers. Lift your hem and let me see the state of your slippers!"

Her voice had a shrill, angry quality, like one of those dogs bred to be very small—all of who resent their stature and take it out on the rest of the world at every opportunity. Phinia backed up somewhat and lifted her skirts.

"Phinia, do not expose your ankles so shamelessly," the lady added.

"But Mama—"

"Do not 'but Mama' me. Duke Carly is preparing a luncheon repast in our honor and I will not have you appearing before your fiancé looking like a fishwife. Bad enough that you comport yourself like one. Durrin, we shall have words about your allowing the princess to consort with a man of such strange and disreputable appearance. Phinia, it is *bad enough* that I find you out here playing in the dirt with servants and..."

The lady was obviously searching for some noun suitable to cover Xeras's ostensible disrepute, and temporarily coming up short. Her husband seemed grateful for this logjam in her verbosity.

"If you could come and join us in our suite, daughter," he said. "And if this gentleman has some expertise with dragons, perhaps he might join us."

A quick glance around showed Phinia's face brighten, her mother's flush beet red and Durrin's become suggestive of advanced degree of indigestion.

Kick the damn horse, darkling. Get us out of here!

Xeras, with perhaps an excess of vigor, complied. The horse's head shot up, its ears lay down and, with a jolt of anticipation, Xeras felt its muscles bunch up beneath him.

Xeras's whole body rocked back and he released the reins to grab desperately for the saddle horn. And they were off.

ᙅᙆ

It had never occurred to Xeras that in the course of moving quickly forward a horse also does a hell of a lot of emphatic bouncing up and down. With every step, he lifted out of the saddle and lurched in some arbitrary direction as the fates decreed, then slammed back down. Finally he locked his legs onto the barrel of the horse's body and clung to the pommel, thumping around so his teeth clacked together and all the mysterious internal parts of his body seemed to be having a barn dance.

Hang on tight!

"Gee, thanks, Drin. I would never have thought of that!"

The horse's hooves hammered on the flagstones of the street as they shot through town. The jolting blur made no sense. Closing his eyes made it even more terrifying but there wasn't much to do but hope he would stay attached to the saddle which would in turn stay attached to the horse. Eventually the forward motion slowed while the up and down stuff got even worse. Finally a gait he could understand, some sensible walking. The horse ambled a little farther and stopped, craning its neck to peer back at him for a belated consultation.

"Don't look at me like that. This wasn't really what I had in mind."

The horse snorted and started grazing the scrubby grass at its feet. It had gone back to assuming it didn't have to pay any attention to him. Everything hurt, his butt from slamming in the saddle, his tongue which had been bitten, his heart, thudding fast and hollow. Shaking he slipped both feet out of the stirrups, lifted one leg over in front of him, then jumped down. He leapt away from the animal and glared at it accusingly. The horse did not even deign to acknowledge the action.

They stood in a small lane that dwindled and disappeared up a steep hill ahead of them. He could see a few dry-stone walls, some straggling shrubbery. His first ample meal for a long stretch was not sitting well; it took some effort to hold onto it at all. Xeras leaned against a tall stone that stood by the track, feeling sour saliva well up in his mouth. The horse moved on to nibble at some overhanging foliage, but did not seem to like the taste. It glanced at him again with bemused, if oversized, innocence.

The poor thing thought it was doing what you wanted, darkling.

Xeras sat on the ground, resting his back against the stone. As if the horse were the height of his problems...

"When are you going to stop haunting me, Drin? What's the point of it really?"

Maybe when you settle down with some sensible young man. Not to steal from beneath the little princess's nose, but this Duke Carly surely fits the bill. You like him, he likes you, and it's quite simple.

Which was Drin all over. Not so much a vengeful spook as a spectral matchmaker. Xeras checked to make sure nobody was nearby. The nice villagers weren't exactly racing to ensure he was all right. They could hardly have failed to notice his gallop through town. Raising his tunic, he saw the greenish, fluid-filled bump just to the side of his belly button.

"Oh yes, my life is very simple," he agreed. "I just need to settle down with a man who's destined to be supper for a dragon to raise our bouncing baby monster here—one which I will give birth to by some method I'd rather not know about right now—and then life will be nothing but smooth sailing and beautiful sunsets."

You don't know that was a vision, with Carly and the dragon. You've had bad dreams before.

"And how is it that you know what I dreamed?"

I see what you see, I know what you know and I feel what you feel. Even when you won't admit it, Xeras, and am here with you and for you. My days of knowing the world any way but through you are over. And when I am satisfied you can go on without me, I will leave.

Xeras laughed bitterly. "I am going on without you. This isn't making it easier, it's making it harder." As he said it that didn't sound quite true, but Xeras clenched his mouth shut over an elaboration. If Drin truly was some kind of restless spirit, he didn't want to stand in the way of him going to his reward.

A sort of general thoughtful silence descended. Drin kept quiet for once. The horse grazed on the ragged grasses, clanking its metal bit. The day wended along, the sun crawling across the sky. By and by, Xeras felt a bit more settled, in his body at least. He looked down at the bump again, running his thumb over it.

You're not going to kill it.

"You think it's your place to tell me that."

Would that I could tell you anything, darkling. You never were a biddable one. That's not what I mean. There's a chance, a pretty good chance, it could hurt you. I'd see it dead a hundred times over before taking that chance. But you're not going to kill it. You're just never going to want to see another creature die in your life, not for any reason. It's not something that's in your

57

head, it's in your heart and you've walled yourself off so hard from your own feelings you can barely hear them at all except through my voice. You don't know it yet, but you will never be able to make yourself do it.

"Is that what you are, the voice of my heart?"

Our heart. You gave it to me and so I cannot help but live here. Until, perhaps, you give it to another. And I hope you will, Xeras. I have other places to be. And I can't be here and there both.

Xeras closed his eyes. That was quite the monologue from Drin. He'd been passing comments for some weeks now, but just a quip here, an aside, a flippant remark. In the darkness behind Xeras's eyelids another darkness lurked—the darkness of a cell. In the shadows a naked body lay curled, just the faintest outlines of his wasted limbs discernable by light that came in through a small window in the corridor behind them. The longer he stood the clearer his vision became.

"You are here to witness the penalty," his father said. "To an end to this aberration and move on with your life as a scion of Tirrin, of the Soun line and heritage of which you are sole heir."

Xeras had moved forward slowly, kneeling beside the low bench. It was Drin's body, he was dead and without pulse—but life had fled so recently that Drin's body was still warmer than the chill of the cell. Xeras stayed by his side until he realized that this was not how he wanted to remember Drin. Drin was gone. All the anguish, the protests and the drawn out, pitiful end—like water running from a broken vessel—the man he knew had gone and only emptiness remained. He stood, turned and walked past his father and the other nobles clustered outside. He walked to the port and spent all the coin in his pockets for a berth on a boat heading for the mainland. He got off that boat and kept on walking. Everything since that was little more than a blur...

The horse had been working its way back to him. Now it bumped its muzzle roughly against his shoulder.

"I guess it's time I stopped running, and here is as good as any place. What do you think?"

Are you addressing me or the horse?

"That depends on which one is going to give me the most sensible answer."

You stick with that horse, kid. Silence is often the best sense a man can get.

"Oh, irony of ironies," Xeras muttered. But he stood with a fragile feeling of peace, ready to see what, if anything, awaited him back at the duke's house.

Chapter Six

Xeras did take a tour around town, such as it was, first—and a good bit of the surrounding area. A nice enough place, but small and everything was built in a way that suggested things got very cold for a good part of the year. The part coming very soon. A few sullen traders labored up the hill and through town, paying their toll with a grumble at the huge gate he had mistaken for a bridge.

Walking along the main road, Xeras regarded the gate that rose up behind the town. It jutted from the raw rock. The gate was an imposing structure—maybe the height of two hundred men to get to the top. And it looked like there might be a path at the top, a path like the one under Carly's feet in that dream. It was hard to imagine any other foothold above the town on the sheer cliffs around them. The gate capitalized, quite literally, on a single narrow pass that certainly appeared to be the only good way through the mountain range for some distance. Its sheer size suggested the involvement of magic; surely no purely mechanical device could operate it?

Xeras held the reins gingerly and the horse followed calmly enough. He learned to give it a good length of rein, because of the way its head bobbed up and down with each step. By the time they turned into the stable, the horse was going first. He fumbled with the gate and managed to get his horse inside its stall without letting the other one out. Largely because the other one didn't want out.

He was struggling with far too many buckles and straps of his associates' equine accessories when a foot kicked at the other side the stall door.

"How far did he take you?"

"Oh, there and back again."

"I am glad about the back again at least." Carly leant his elbow upon the stall door and his chin upon his hand. He was clearly amused, but in a friendly way.

"You're quick to become partial to people, my lord Duke."

And you're quick to piss on a gift. Try unwrapping it instead. Just forget I'm here. I promise not to peek.

Everything else aside, Carly could hardly avoid getting an eyeful of the dragon junior if things went the way Drin was hinting. Now that was a conversation he was in no hurry to have. Xeras pulled free another buckle and all that happened was the stirrup strap felt loose and the metal stirrup tumbled to the ground.

Carly slipped into the stall. "You really have no idea what you're doing, do you?"

Too true.

The duke stripped off the horse's bridle, then the heavy saddle which he laid over the door. As he did so he mused, "It makes me wonder if there might be a few other things that you don't have a lot of experience with. Because that might explain why you are quite so jumpy. Although it does beg the question of just what you *have* been doing with your life up 'til now."

Xeras loitered in the corner of the stall and watched. Carly had a good muscular body and his face revealed only amiable humor. He was asking if his attention was welcome or unwanted; Xeras kind of wished he had an answer to that. But as a preliminary position it seemed safer not to lead the man on, regardless of Drin's counsel on the matter.

"I had a peculiar upbringing," Xeras said. "But there are still limits to my ignorance, and also—though you might find it hard to believe—to your appeal."

Carly laughed, brushing the gelding down. "You're not the first to say so. But I do have a way of growing on people sometimes."

Xeras grimaced; the turn of phrase was an unfortunate one.

"No?" Carly said. "Well, I dare say my pride could do with being whittled down a little, 'tis my sister's opinion anyway." He reached out, hand musty with the smell of leather and horse sweat, and touched Xeras's stubbled cheek with just the back of one fingertip—stroking down once and pulling back. "That Thurstian duke still wants to talk to you. They have a dragon trouble of their own. They might let up on me if you go and take a look at their overgrown lizard."

Xeras, don't you dare. Plegura's the only one of them with morning-after angst. You're nothing but a light snack for the rest of the dragon race.

Perversely that made him more sure that he wanted to do it. "So you're not interested in the porcelain princess? She appears to be a nice enough child."

"I'm not looking to adopt any more than I'm looking to marry. I'm just saying that if you and their man Durrin head up the north hill and see what you can do about their dragon, then Durrin will come back this way and escort young Phinia home— and in the meantime the royal couple will leave me in peace. Not that I have the faintest idea yet what it is with you and dragons, so if you'd rather not?"

Xeras looked at Carly with incredulity. "They are leaving the girl here? But going back themselves?"

"The duke said she seemed to be enjoying herself here—apparently that is unusual."

"Ha. That must be some dragon."

Xeras let himself out of the stall. Carly followed, delayed a little as he set the bolt back. "What do you mean?"

"They're obviously hoping it'll eat me."

"I don't understand. I mean for start, they're sending their man with you."

"The duchess, at least, is hoping it'll eat him too. In either case, you'll have spent an extended period with an unchaperoned young lady. From their point of view, you'll have to marry her. You may have to tell me what a Ballot Duke is, after all. Because I am curious to know by what process you were left in charge of this place."

C3

Xeras, you may hesitate to consummate the young man's desires, but must you really insult him?

Xeras shook his head, trying to drive off the chiding voice. Carly led him into a spacious parlor. A fierce hearth fire roared, and many candles were dotted about the room, mounted in sconces on the wall and a large, branched candelabra. Two ladies in livery stood to the side of the great mantle, Limry and the younger woman he had seen that morning. Durrin was there too, albeit standing as far away from the others as he could get without jumping out the window. Seated about the fire were Katinka upon a wing-backed chair and the visiting Thurstians upon one long bench, the duchess and princess with busywork in their hands and the duke inspecting his empty goblet glumly.

Seeing Xeras, both father and daughter seemed to brighten, although the duchess's mouth twisted as if she tasted something bitter. Katinka didn't look too pleased either, but apparently for another reason.

"Brother, dear," she said. "Did you truly agree that Phinia should stay behind while Durrin and our new retainer go a-dragon hunting? You do realize that after one night without a Thurstian chaperone you would be counted as having wed her?"

"I thank you for enlightening me on that point, dearest sister. Our noble guests were not so considerate. Needless to say, Phinia will return with her parents." Carly strode into the circle of flickering light cast by the flames in the deep stone hearth and the wax-dripping candelabra. Xeras felt strangely reluctant and hung back in the shadows. Xeras was somewhat distracted by being referred to as a "retainer". It sounded rather proprietary.

"But you have agreed," the duchess snapped. "Given your word as a man of honor."

"An agreement based on deception is no agreement," Carly said, quite without recrimination. "Just as a marriage not based on love is not a marriage. It has been our great pleasure to have you with us, but I feel you must have matters to attend to back in Thurst, and I wouldn't want to separate you from your lovely daughter for as much as a moment. As you say, she is an extraordinary girl and you will no doubt be pleased not to be parted from her."

Any other man might have been angry at the attempt to force him into betrothal. Carly was not even chiding in his response. He emanated an indulgent benevolence that no ill will or low trick could puncture. Xeras was altogether alarmed at how he was beginning to feel about the man who possessed so many virtues emphatically absent from his own character.

"Is it yellow?" Xeras asked. The assembled company looked at him quite blankly. "The dragon in Thurst," Xeras added slowly. "Is it, in color, yellow?"

The Thurstian duke replied eagerly. "It is for the most part yellow, on its head and limbs, but more orange or brown upon the body. Why do you ask?"

"I think, perhaps, I should meet this dragon," Xeras concluded. Whatever reservations he might have about ending up in the man's bed, it would be good to prevent Carly's fate as dragon bait. If such a thing was possible. Never having evinced a talent for prophecy, it was not an area in which he was trained.

"You sound as if you actually expect to converse with the monster," the duchess mocked.

"Is that how it works?" asked her husband. "Do dragons speak?"

"...and what was that language you spoke to the one you call Plegura?" Katinka added.

They were all but drowned out by Drin. *I absolutely forbid it, Xeras. You are not going near any more dragons. Do you hear me? You got lucky in more ways than one when you encountered Plegura. You should deal with that little problem before throwing yourself in the way of enormous carnivorous lizards. The next one might be less lascivious and more peckish!*

In listening to Drin, Xeras realized he had stood, ignoring the living people present for a long and probably awkward moment. He looked down sharply at a ring of faces and addressed Katinka.

"I was speaking *dragon*, of course." He considered that this omened future he had dreamed might be coming up any night.

65

No reason to dally. "If your man, Durrin, can show me the way, we should go at once. I dare say that yellow dragon should not be left to do as it wishes any longer than is necessary."

"Xeras," Carly said. "This creature is up in the high mountains between our two realms and snow is on the way. And you, apparently, do not even know how to ride. Perhaps we should form a larger party; I could..."

"No, Durrin can show the way. Otherwise I will go alone."

Listen to the man. If it is too dangerous to allow him to go, how can it be sane for, and I say this with love, a fumble butt like you? I really must put my foot down.

It seemed unlikely that Drin had much in the way of anatomy at all, let alone feet, but it was hard to disregard the edge of panic growing in the phantom's voice.

Carly sat on the second bench. "I am the duke. If you are to swear allegiance to me, it would be nice to see some indication that you will do my bidding."

Xeras straightened his back. He had little in the way of breadth, but considerably more height than anyone in the room. "I accepted an offer of employment. I swear allegiance, I give unquestioning obedience to no man. As we have discussed, although I am most dreadfully ignorant in many areas, I do seem to be the only one here who knows how to converse with dragons. And that is exactly what I intend to do. Or would you have your near neighbors continue to suffer from the creature's depredations?"

Carly and his sister looked up at him with mild interest, as if finding a familiar pet could do a trick they did not recall teaching to it. Only Phinia seemed enthralled by his little display of pique, which was enough to make him feel foolish. And the duchess smiled. He had no idea what she was thinking, but the expression was about as reassuring as watching a serpent smile at a rat and probably had a similar meaning.

"To avoid any difficulty, I think my good husband and I should remain here. And await the gentleman's return, and that of our retainer," she said. "Naturally Phinia would stay with us. That would avoid any appearance of impropriety whilst the duke's man here investigates our problematical, uh, creature."

"Dragon," her husband added. "A very big one."

"Yes, dear, *thank you.* I was, of course, aware of that."

"You would, I hope," Katinka added, "try to converse with it from some distance away. In case it proves not to be, ah, sociable."

"*I'd* like to know what you said to the green one," Carly said. "To make it run away from you like that."

"It was something along the lines of 'hello'," Xeras admitted. "I can have that effect on a lady."

☙

The conversation went on into the night. Xeras drifted about the room, running his hand along the shelves where dusty books and weapons lay haphazardly. Carly and the duchess carried most of the argument. Well, the duchess sounded like she was arguing no matter what she said. Carly continued to respond to her with good humor. Xeras didn't concern himself overly with the details. He was going to look for the dragon with the yellow arm, whatever they might decide.

Drin hissed at him. ...*not some kind of mythical hero, Xeras. You have many, well some, fine qualities, but whenever you get your hands on something sharp, you cut yourself, and whenever you get hold of something heavy, you drop it on your foot. Look what happened when you got on the back of a horse for Gods' sake!*

And a great deal more in this general vein. Xeras looked up to find Phinia watching him with wide eyes. Katinka watched Phinia with a slight frown. Carly, in turn, kept his eyes on Katinka with his usual benign interest—and finally the cat's cradle was completed by the duchess. She surveyed Xeras speculatively.

"If Seras is quite confident the dragon will not harm him..." Katinka said.

Xeras wondered if they had been acquainted too long for a correction of pronunciation to be considered polite. And as to her implied question, he need only tell the monster he was pregnant. Dragons would not hurt him then, surely? Not given what the big grey one had said about their small numbers and limited chances to propagate. It was a worrying that an excuse to keep Plegura's spawn alive a little longer came as something of a relief. But he would need the little tadpole to ensure the dragon would not harm him.

That hardly seems a well-reasoned supposition for a man educated in both rhetoric and philosophy.

But Carly echoed the ghost's concerns. "Seras, are you quite sure the dragon will respond...courteously to your approaches?"

Xeras rubbed his temple with irritation. "I don't think it would be likely to eat me after I have introduced myself. It would not be polite."

"This is a beast that has eaten not just our livestock. A number of men and women from more distant homesteads are also unaccounted for," Phinia said. "You would be terribly careful, I hope? And you are, um, quite sure about that?"

"I will be terribly careful." Xeras stayed carefully silent on the second point.

To the extent that you are terrible at being careful, Drin muttered grimly.

Carly and Katinka exchanged glances but seemed inclined to give him the benefit of the doubt. Xeras resolved to keep his mouth shut when it came to his reasoning, knowing that the real facts might bring an abrupt end to that indulgence.

Chapter Seven

Xeras had gone to his rest feeling quite pleased with himself. He had the dream; he was offered a way to stop it from happening. That was the way it worked, surely? What would be the point of prophecy otherwise? Unless the Gods were rather more cruel than most people cared to believe.

But he couldn't think of sleeping until he dredged up a plan for reasoning with or, if necessary, doing away with the yellow dragon. There was rather a lack of furniture in his room. Even the bathtub had been emptied and carried off. So he sat on the bed to muse it over.

During his solitary childhood, Xeras had read many of the dusty tomes in the great libraries of Tirrin. On one particular occasion, he had come across a few slim journals that discussed or were reputed to be actually written by dragons. The subject had caught his imagination, even though these creatures lived far away and some said they did not exist at all. Their tongue was known to a few old scholars who received little but derision for perpetuating a tongue probably dead and possibly nothing more than an elaborate invention.

However, to be counted as a scholar himself, Xeras had needed to become proficient in a rare language as part of the small nation's plan to retain all of its academic resources. Dragon-speech suited his interest in obscure knowledge, his disinterest in conversation, and drove his father most satisfyingly livid with rage at the pointlessness and ridiculous nature of the endeavor. But it was an exercise he had completed and been done with quite some years ago. He was unsure how much of it he could bring to mind now.

He only hoped he could draw it up from the depths of memory, given a little time. He tried to visualize the books he had studied so carefully. One was written in dragon tongue that contained a passage, he was sure, that referred to an agreement between dragons and men. He had read it many times when trying to improve his fluency in a language few others knew and none spoke well. Closing his eyes to bring the chapped and faded cover of the first book to mind, and then the first page…

☙

There exists a particular sort of confusion experienced by a man who becomes aware he is waking up, but was not aware that he had fallen asleep in the first place. In this case Xeras was further confounded by a disquieting, heavy sensation in his chest that made it difficult to breathe. He opened his eyes and looked down at the top of a head from which profuse, pallid hair grew. He closed his eyes again. Phinia.

What was the princess doing on his bed, lying across him to a degree that he could feel the slight mound of her breast pressing against his side? He opened his mind to any possible explanation and was rewarded with a sort of fuzzy confusion like the sound of the sea in a very large shell. Maybe if he kept his eyes shut she would go away? That seemed like better advice for dealing with bears than princesses.

If you don't get the right person in your bed, one way or another, you tend to end up with the wrong one.

Xeras gritted his teeth together. As much as he wanted to curse the ghost's unconstructive commentary, he would rather avoid waking the princess. It couldn't possibly get much more "wrong" than this. In the still of the early morning, he could hear a distant sound, a thud and the faint cadences of the dulcet duchess. Xeras had a nasty intuition as to what had put a bee in her bonnet first thing in the day.

Her missing daughter, perhaps?

Thank you, Drin, Master of the Obvious. Peering down, Xeras perceived that said missing daughter wore nothing more than her shift. In contrast with her daywear, this was a rather insubstantial garment. And even for one inclined to admire feminine attributes, she had little to boast of in that department as yet. Much of her curves, it seemed, were a virtue of dressing making rather than anatomy.

Sayeth the man who looks like he was assembled out of broom handles.

Drin was not put off by having his commentary go unacknowledged. Xeras nudged Phinia and she stretched out along his body and looked up at him drowsily. Free of paints and powders, she looked rather pretty, and very young indeed.

"You are going to get dressed now," he said tersely.

"But Sir Seras, I've chosen to give myself to you. But when I came to you, you were already asleep," she said with mild reproof. Xeras just wasn't living up to his half of whatever poetry-inspired fantasy had motivated her actions.

"Get dressed, now," Xeras repeated, slowly and carefully so as not to be misunderstood, as he extracted himself from bed and princess both.

"But I could hardly... I didn't dare try and put on a dress before I left. It is nearly impossible without the help of a servant anyway." She sat up on the bed and raised her arms. "I came as

I am."

I wouldn't call that underdeveloped. Rather pleasing, actually.

The girl's sleeping shift bordered on, no, it actually was pretty indecent. Despite being narrower in his taste than the lascivious Drin, Xeras averted his eyes. "Use that blanket, then. I'm taking you back."

"Don't you love me?"

Something deep inside Xeras flinched even at the word. "Phinia, child, I don't how you could have gotten that idea."

"I just..." There was a ruffling sound. "You can look now."

If the princess had looked glum yesterday morning, now she was truly distraught. Tears pooled in her freakishly large eyes and she was curled up with the blanket pulled over her shoulder and clutched roughly at the corner by her tiny, white hands.

"I just thought because I felt it for you, you must feel it for me. I thought that was just how it worked."

"You don't even know me."

Obviously, darkling. Or she would know better.

"Oh, for Gods' sake, not now, Drin."

Shit. He'd never done that before, slipped enough to talk to the damn apparition while somebody was right next to him. Xeras hoped that if he ignored it, Phinia would too. He went with a sigh to sit by her side. Phinia leaned against him tentatively like a timid dog. So, she thought love only happened if it was mutual. Wouldn't the world be a better place if that were so.

"The soul knows, doesn't it, when you find your mate?" she asked. "That's what love is."

He put one arm around her, feeling for the first time in his life like the older, wiser person in a conversation. "When love goes well it is on both sides. But it often goes astray. That's why it is wise to know about a person by the usual methods rather than rely on your soul's uncertain wisdom. Souls can be a little...hopeful, sometimes."

"Then you are saying—"

"That it is time we got you back to your parents."

"But they'll know I was gone all night. If you will not marry me, I'll be ruined."

And with that she began to cry, messily and in earnest. Xeras didn't really feel the pitch of sympathy that such a display should evoke. He was concerned, certainly, but how heartbroken could she be after such a short time?

"If they knew you were gone all night," Xeras mused. "Why are they only looking for you now?"

"They thought I was with Duke Carly. That is what they wanted."

"I think it's pretty clear what they wanted."

Like a pig to mud, a teenager is drawn to do the one thing her parents would not want her to do.

The duchess's voice could still be very dimly heard, like a small insect in the distance. Or a large insect at a very large distance—in any case not something you'd want to get any closer to. With a sigh Xeras, reached one hand out to Phinia. "So, we are going back to your room," he said.

"What shall we say to my mother?"

"The truth, of course. There is a certain power to the truth, no matter how unlikely it might seem."

Phinia sniffled and looked up at him skeptically. Yes, well, in some areas he was no doubt even more naïve than her. But they couldn't sit here all day and hope the duchess suffered from an apoplexy. And just because the princess followed him home, he certainly wasn't going to keep her. That left one other option.

☙

The princess took him to the guest suite on the second floor and near the front of the house.

Just make another run for it, Xeras. Honestly.

He wasn't sure if Drin was serious or not. The door to the suite was ajar and a great commotion was in progress within. Xeras leaned to peer through the gap and Phinia, in front of him, did the same.

"If your household cannot keep my daughter safe," the duchess declared, somewhat hoarsely, "then perhaps I made a mistake in pursuing this match in the first place."

Katinka's normally equanimity seemed a little strained. "It was not an aspect of our nations' alliance that my brother ever wished to develop, my lady. As soon as we locate the princess, we will be happy to see you safely to our mutual border."

"If he truly disapproved, he should not have met with Phinia last night, should he?" the duchess replied triumphantly. "Do not think I was misled, young man. Your apparent indifference was clearly a bargaining position in relation to the dowry. But you cannot have it both ways."

"Carly did not meet with your daughter, this or any other night. If she has chosen to leave these rooms, which you—I must point out—shared with her, that is hardly a matter under our control."

Phinia tried to back away from the room, but Xeras put one hand on her shoulder and reached for the door with the other.

He had a little trouble finding the impetus necessary to draw everyone's attention and weather the inevitable flurry of hysteria.

"If you are suggesting my daughter would behave in any way that is improper," the duchess continued in full voice. "Well, I demand that you retract any such insinuation. I absolutely demand it."

"Now dear," her husband interjected, but his objection was quickly rolled over. He looked up and saw Xeras and Phinia through the gap in the door, apparently the only one in the room to notice them.

"In fact," the duchess declared, "if you did not know exactly where the princess was, why then you would be looking for her, wouldn't you? I know you have her secreted away somewhere because you intend to keep her without a proper matrimony."

The lady was more concerned about being stolen from than the safety of her daughter. A flash of annoyance on the girl's behalf helped him finally step forward. Xeras pushed Phinia ahead into the room, reaching over her head to open the door fully.

"I hear that somebody mislaid a princess; I think I might be able to help out there," he said.

To his surprise, Phinia immediately burst into a resurgence of explosive weeping and ran into her father's arms, which, added to her state of near undress led to some rather suspicious looks all around.

"He doesn't love me," she snorted wetly into the Thurstian duke's shoulder.

"Phinia, we did talk about that," Xeras said weakly.

"You are on first-name terms with my daughter," the duchess said with an uncharacteristic lack of volume that was somehow even more threatening than her previous vapors.

"Seras, did you?" Katinka asked. "I mean you and the princess." She made a vague gesture that suggested her two hands were getting to know each other intimately.

"No," Xeras said in horror. "I woke up and she was there. If I were given to wooing princesses, let alone successfully, my life would be a lot more like the one my father planned for me."

Do you regret meeting me, darkling?

Drin never did take into account that Xeras was interacting with the living here and not really able to engage in a serious, simultaneous conversation with the dead. But Xeras didn't want to leave it alone either. If there was one thing, just one thing, that he actually didn't regret about his life, it was meeting Drin.

You can just think *your reply, you know. It's not like I have ears anymore either.*

"I don't think it's the *wooing* the good duchess is concerned with," Carly added, blithely calm as usual. "As much as the, well, consummating."

"Actually," the Thurstian duke interjected nervously. "If they have lain in the same bed with no other person in the room to vouch for Phinia's honor, consummation is deemed to have occurred. The boy must marry her." And, strangely, he didn't seem particularly averse to the idea.

Everyone looked from him to Xeras, and back again.

I do so love a wedding.

"You people manage to make the dragons look sane and reasonable." Xeras turned and left the room. If he had hoped to find folk outside of Tirrin to be more reasonable and less rule-bound, it appeared he was going to be disappointed.

 files

It was raining, again. Not heavily, but with persistence and some of the gusts were flecked with flakes of snow that built on the ground in a dirty, speckled slush. Xeras stood in the stable, leaning on the stall door. The big tawny horse, his associate from the previous day, came over and rested its hairy chin on his shoulder, snorting wetly on Xeras's ear. He began to think the horse for all its vagaries was, after all, the most sensible individual he had met in this town. He heard someone approaching, and turned to see Carly.

"What are you going to do?" Carly asked.

"If you don't object to me borrowing this horse, I am going to go speak with that yellow dragon."

Extremely yellow, one must hope.

"How do you expect to find it, exactly?"

"So far they have demonstrated a knack of finding me."

Carly laughed, a deep chuckle that burst out like he'd been holding it in. It didn't seem like the duke was going to march Xeras off to a precipitous handfasting to the princess. "I'd choose a dragon over the duchess as a mother-in-law, too. I'll even come along."

"No!"

That drew a raised eyebrow from Carly, but this was the last thing Xeras expected a responsible functionary like the duke to say. Xeras scoured his mind for a convincing excuse, but failed to come up with anything more plausible than the quite inadequate truth. Then it occurred to him. If the dragon seized Carly from the top of the great gate, it should not matter if Carly got closer to the dragon so long as he got correspondingly distant from the gate. The prophecy could presumably only come to pass if all three came together. With no clear certainty of the dragon's position, separating Carly from the gate was in fact the most rational thing to do.

"All right then," Xeras amended blithely. "Yes."

"I am beginning to think you take pride in being contrary," Carly said mildly.

"It would make him a good match for our Phinia," said a third voice from the doorway.

It was the Duke of Thurst, Kellof, a smiling and intensely benign man, ambling over with the rolling gait of a habitual horseman. He addressed himself to Carly. "My good wife, you see, understands that this man of yours is of a high house of Tirrin, and that any man carrying the true blood of Tirrin cannot help but be a formidable ally."

Xeras felt cold. He stood and looked over the stall door at the horse. And the horse, with some apparent, sympathy looked back. It did not surprise him that the duchess would be an admirer of the Tirrin nobility. They were vicious, status-conscious tyrants on a scale she could only aspire too—and apparently did.

"Your lady wife is mistaken," Xeras said blandly.

"She is, I am excruciatingly aware, many less-than-admirable things, but I must say that *mistaken* is rarely one of them. And having been acquainted with several emissaries of Tirrin, we have both become acquainted with their appearance. The mien and to some extent the manner of Tirrinian, is, ah, distinctive."

"That is not the matter on which she is mistaken." Xeras turned to Carly. "If you wish to be part of this errand, is there any reason to delay?"

It would have the benefit of making your life a day or two longer, or even an hour...

"The trade season is closing and the winter will be here

soon," Carly said. "If we are to go, it needs must be immediately. But I do have to think of my guests."

"Oh," the Thurstian duke responded. "We expect heavy snow within days; I had best return to Thurst to see to the tiresome administrative duties attached to my title. But I have long since given up hope of predicting the duchess's actions, let alone attempting to influence them. She may prefer to lie in wait, determining which of you would be a better match for Phinia and making the necessary arrangements. We have four daughters, you understand, as well as two sons. My lady wife has become willing to be rather speculative in some of their matches. A democratic duke or an itinerant Tirrinian—she might take some time in deciding."

Both dukes shared a most irritating equanimity about their own fates and the fates of others. Peculiar, but Xeras found their very refusal to be perturbed most irritating.

"Do you happen to have a preference?" Carly asked conversationally.

Kellof laughed. "Phinia is the very picture of her mother in her youth. She will do well enough regardless, once she gets away from the duchess. If I were you I would get on with that dragon hunt and let the ladies do as they will. It is not as if we really have a choice in the matter."

Chapter Eight

The duchess had a gift for inspiring alacrity in others. It was still morning when the Duke of Thurst directed his hack down the path with a cheerful wave. For a man of rotund form and frame, and diffident manner, he wasn't at all worried about a horseback journey of several days with the temperature plummeting. In fact he was obviously looking forward to it.

Durrin stayed with the duchess, and was rather less cheerful at the prospect. He had volunteered to escort Kellof or even, with a much reduced degree of enthusiasm, Carly. But his role was destined to be no more than placing a mark upon a map showing the dragon's preferred lair up in the rocky hills. The princess, or so her mother declared, required a guard and chaperone. Xeras thought it was that the duchess required someone to be at her own beck and call in lieu of her husband. The carriage remained behind for the convenience the duchess and her youngest daughter so they could return at their leisure, although it seemed the window of opportunity was closing as the weather deteriorated. Katinka watched grimly as their visitors arranged matters in their suite, apparently anticipating an extended stay.

Somewhat later in the morning, Xeras and Carly were seen off by a row of women. The duchess with her arms folded. The diffident princess beside her showed signs of a rapid recovery from her broken heart and had fallen into a sort of "wait and see" attitude. Katinka left them both to stride over to her brother.

"I shall do my best to ensure you have a duchy to return to," she said waspishly. "But don't tarry. I am not happy with this whole idea, brother. You are not a callow boy now with nothing better to do but chase around the hills after adventure. Indeed, you have proved surprisingly competent and would, all things considered, be a loss to the duchy if you fell off one of those sheer cliffs or got too close to a dragon not in the mood to converse."

"It is almost winter," Carly said with good cheer. "Soon there will be nothing by short dull days and long dull nights to spend stopping the men from getting into too many fistfights, feeding the sheep and awaiting the spring. Try and talk the lady into some sense about the honor of her daughter, because one way or the other, she is heading back home on our return, unless"—he cast a look at Xeras—"you could do worse?"

Xeras imagined his expression was sufficient reply.

☙

Rain. Interminable rain with short breaks of sleet or snow and a number of gradations between each of these states. Carly led the way, whistling happily. His indelible good humor was more irritating than the rain. It seemed that any excuse to get out into the countryside came as very welcome to him, although he did not appear to take the matter of conversing with dragons terribly seriously. Xeras's horse followed its partner without need of any input from him, fortunately. He sat, slipping back in the saddle as they wended upwards, feeling the insides of his thighs chafing, his side itch and the rainwater dapple, drench and finally soak through his borrowed cloak and clothes. The bundle of blankets and provisions lashed to the back of his saddle creaked with every movement, but it stopped him from slipping right over the animal's broad rump as they climbed onwards and ever upwards.

With each upward step, he grew colder. Xeras kept his arms clamped over his body and cloak drawn tight around him, it still felt colder than any winter in Tirrin, and here they counted that season as having not yet begun.

If you had any meat on you, it might not bite so deep. As 'tis, a dragon would find you more use as a toothpick than a meal.

Carly craned back. "Finding your seat, I trust?"

"I believe I may be frozen to it."

You could turn around now and still make Ballot's Keep before dark. Your "seat" could be considered more than a token effort, but it would be a pity to freeze what there is of it right off.

Xeras tried to block the general unpleasantness of reality from his mind and recall the tome on dragons. There was mention of an agreement, he was sure, a contract between humans and the mages of Tirrin. Now the mages of Tirrin from that age of empire, even taking into account the exaggerations history tended to accumulate, were described as capable of far greater and more powerful acts than their modern-day descendents. But the agreement might still be in force, in theory, between what remained of those mages and what remained of the dragons who were, if not lesser, certainly fewer. Or at least he hoped it might be as this *theory* was all he had to go on.

He had a good memory, but to dredge up a recollection from so many years ago. He hadn't been all that interested in the contents of the book at the time or he would have paid more attention. He gripped the saddle horn and tried to ignore the way each swaying step the horse took made every organ in his body lurch from fore to aft and back again.

The Bond of Hurn, that was it. The dragons had to respect the beasts and abodes of men and in return, what they had they received in return?

Any chance it was nubile young princesses? Because it looks like you're going to have one of those and you sure don't have any use for her. It's traditional anyway, isn't it? Damsels and dragons?

Drin's sense of humor was wearing a little thin. It was hard to have a complete thought from beginning to end without interruption and besides... Phinia, although no personal friend, was a girl in a difficult position. Xeras was baffled that she would choose to put herself in such a compromising position with him. Could a young girl really develop an infatuation so quickly? Dammit. Xeras's eyes flicked open and he glowered at Carly's broad back ahead of him, above his steed's broad ass. Now was not the time to be thinking about that. He needed to work out some kind of strategy, some way to approach the dragon without ending up on the menu.

He closed his eyes again. His systematic mind fastened on the first page with furious attention. No matter what Drin said, he was determined not to be deflected from his thoughts. It was vital that he dredge the detail of the agreement from his recalcitrant memory. *The Bond of Hurn states that...*

"You sleeping?"

Xeras's drooping head snapped up. He lurched back on the saddle. The horse made a startled harrumph and sidestepped. Before he could react, Xeras toppled off the horse's back. His arms and legs flailed, responding to some misdirected reflexes and ignoring his mind's directions entirely. Carly made a frantic grab for him, but caught no more than a corner of his cloak.

Despite the fact that saddle truly was quite a distance from the ground, he moved from one place to the other pretty much instantaneously.

Xeras's shoulder hit the rocky path, one foot kicking free of the stirrup and the other twisting and catching so he ended up dragged a step or two before the big horse stopped, looked back at him and gave the equine equivalent of a sigh.

That horse has more sense than either of you. He'd probably rather be back in his warm stable.

An experimental jiggle of his leg drew a sharp protesting pain in his knee, but had no other effect. Other parts of his body, arm, shoulder and abraded palm, registered muted agreement with the knee. This was a very uncomfortable position to be in. Finally Carly deigned to come to his aid, loosening the stirrup leather and pulling Xeras's foot free. His expression wasn't much different from the horse's.

Xeras lay back and looked up at the iron-hued sky, blinking as raindrops bounced off his face.

Carly sighed and remarked, "Were you more busy with the princess than you said, to be sleeping on horseback on a track like this? It is generally something only attempted by horsemen more, um, adept."

"I was *not* asleep."

Carly offered him a hand and implicit disbelief. Xeras ignored the gesture as he rolled on his side and got awkwardly to his feet. His knee ached. He winced and eased his weight off it, wavering in his balance, and took note of the steep slope just to his side. Fortunately Carly reached forward to steady him, broad fingers wrapping around his shoulders and eyes meeting his with the intensity of...

Oh, I felt that. Don't tell me you don't like him.

Xeras turned away, hobbling over to his patient steed.

85

"How far do we have to go?"

It didn't make a blind bit of sense. Xeras was being curt and unreasonable, and had been for the full extent of the time he and Carly had been acquainted. But Drin was right. He felt some interest in Carly and it seemed to be returned. Even without knowing Carly, Xeras liked him. More than liked him, as if they had met in a previous life and needed no introductions. In any case, between the duke and the princess, it rather seemed that the trick to attracting both the fairer and the brawnier sex was acting like a complete ass. He wasn't sure how much longer he could put up with *himself* at this rate.

"It will take more than one day to reach the plateau where the dragon is said to live," Carly replied. "Longer perhaps, if we have cause to stop along the way."

Xeras set the foot of his sound leg in the stirrup iron and swung up, ignoring that gentle jibe which he had clearly earned. Carly just shook his head and mounted up, taking the lead again.

The day wore on, the way winding higher, narrower and fainter. The path, such as it was, began to follow the exposed ridgeline with the sparsely vegetated ground dropping sharply away to each side. Xeras eyed the aspect on either side nervously and patted the horse's shoulder.

"Watch where you put those hooves," he advised.

Xeras couldn't get the concentration he needed to remember the treaty. If the whole book was just some clever satire he was going to end up in quite the tight corner. Pretty soon he couldn't think about much beyond his own discomfort. Xeras eyed the increasingly dizzying drop of the earth behind him with passive terror. He placed his trust largely in the horse that proceeded calmly, sure-footed. As Drin said, it probably had more sense than he did.

He started to shake with cold and when that passed, he felt a kind of ache deep in the muscles of his arms and legs that gradually swamped his other aches and pains. Being too cold to shake probably wasn't a good thing. The wet wind slapped his exposed face. He hunched over so the wind would strike the top of his head instead.

Carly looked back. "You all right?"

"Sure."

Other than being in agony and trekking inexorably to almost certain death. Drin sounded rather terse. *Of course you are, just fine. If I were alive, I could shake you. I could grab you and stop you from doing all these foolish things.*

Xeras huddled farther forward, ramming his clubbed-up hands under his armpits.

Stubborn, you always have to be so stubborn. Was there ever a thing you decided to do that you were turned away from? Even once you knew that it was futile or just dead wrong? Was there ever a thing you were told to do that you did not strive to oppose, even when it was something you wanted? Even to save your life?

Ignoring Drin was something he'd proved unable to do, twice. He hadn't been able to ignore Drin in the flesh and he couldn't ignore his ghost. And truly, somewhere along that rocky path he realized he did believe this voice was Drin's. Somehow he had trapped his lover here on earth, rather than letting him pass over to whatever awaited beyond mortal life. It was just one more misery added to the pile, but perhaps also one true quest.

He had to discover how to release Drin.

And by some method other, please, than your death.

CƷ

By the time it grew dark they were well above the tree line. The rain faltered to a halt but the wind howled constantly, gusting around the rocks. Carly pointed up ahead to a narrow pass between the jagged hills.

"Just through there we should find a barren plateau. Durrin says it is at the far edge of that expanse that the dragon dwells."

Xeras could barely raise his neck to look, all the sinews in his body clenched tight and stuck that way.

"We should stop here," Carly added. "It is the last good cover to be had."

He swung down and led his horse between some large boulders that had broken from the mountain's side. Hopefully not something that happened too often. Xeras's own mount followed along as he had all day, bless him.

Carly set about the tasks that were called for. Stripping tack from his horse, setting hobbles, slinging a feedbag over its head. He unrolled the blankets and laid them in the lee of the cliff. "Get down off there."

"I'm thinking that over." Xeras felt like a golem made of ice; he suspected that if he moved, parts of his body might well drop off and shatter on the ground.

"You've already amply demonstrated that you can't sleep in the saddle." Carly seemed his usual self, not even particularly tired. No doubt he could have made the journey in a day or less, alone. He came over and laid his hand over Xeras's thigh. His eyes fell on Xeras's fingers, where they were curled in a death grip over the saddle horn. "Should have gotten you some gloves." Not that the duke needed them himself. "Now let's be having you."

He reached out in an inviting gesture that Xeras was drawn to in more ways than one. As he eased his right foot out of the stirrup, his twisted knee made sharp protest. Then mustering his courage, he swung over and off. Not taking into account this meant his weight would go down on his injured leg, which made not the slightest effort to support him. Carly grasped him by the waist and steadied him as he wrenched his left foot from the stirrup and leaned against the horse to stay upright.

"Does this horse have a name?" Xeras asked. He had to say something, anything, and that felt like a harmless choice.

Because that's the most important thing right now, getting properly introduced to the beasts of burden.

"We tend to call him Lefty. That's the position he takes in drawing the coach." Carly hovered close as Xeras hobbled over to the blanket laid on the ground. He wasn't going to be much help, he could hardly move. Something Carly did not fail to notice.

"You should have told me."

Like complaints would have helped. There wasn't anything either of them could do about it. Xeras had never been a rough, hale sportsman, and leaving a life of privilege had broken him down more than it had toughened him up. But Xeras did not protest as he was aided in sitting on the slightly damp blanket over a plethora of rocks, leaving Carly to look after Lefty. The two big horses shuffled together into the partial shelter of an overhang and chewed systematically through their ration. Night fell swiftly as the last sliver of sun vanished over the lofty horizon.

Xeras lay on his side, resting his head on his arm. The Bond of Hurn, he recalled, by which the dragons promise not to harass...or the beast of their domiciles...so long as there lives one of each race...who remembers... Remembers what?

If one assumed, as appeared safe, that dragons did exist, then why had the mages of Tirrin formed this agreement? Had there once been dragons living along the coasts and on the islands, dragons whose depredations had to be curbed? Maybe when their numbers dropped, the agreement fell out of use, but how would it drop out of the knowledge of the scholars and archivists of Tirrin? That seemed unlikely given propensity for record keeping and administration the conclave exhibited...

He wasn't sure how much time passed before Carly settled down behind him. The duke pulled at Xeras's cloak. "Trust me on this. We'll put the dry blanket around us and the cloaks over the top."

Xeras didn't grumble as Carly arranged things to his satisfaction. He did feel the solid body against his back, rather close against it.

Who remembers what, dammit? That was the key to the agreement. To enforce it, he had to know what the agreement was. What exactly was meant to be remembered by the men who made the original bond with the dragons.

"You're cold," Carly said.

"You're not the first to remark on it," Xeras muttered. It was the best he could manage by way of apology.

You call that foreplay?

What the hell did...then Carly's muscular arm reached over him as the duke embraced him tightly. "It is always cold up here."

"I can tell," Xeras observed. "You're quite obviously frozen *stiff.*"

Carly's hand reached around, burrowing under Xeras's sodden tunic and lifting it up. Xeras shifted uneasily, pulling the arm under him around to cover the damn dragon spawn. He could feel Carly's altogether hard body touching lightly against his own.

"If you don't want me to be trying anything, then I'm not. The state of my body notwithstanding."

"I wouldn't want anything to get frostbite," Xeras conceded.

Finally, albeit without much charm. I'm not looking, I swear. I'm not even listening—la la la la...

Hardly the most ideal of situations, but the touch, a body against his; Xeras wanted it, despite himself. "I know a way to keep it warm."

"Do you." Carly snuggled in. He ventured to pull up Xeras's tunic far enough to touch skin.

Xeras was suspended between the desire to be touched, to be held, and disbelief that he was inviting this. His body still ached and his sodden feet were freezing cold, but he burned, too. He dimly felt Drin's presence, although not his regard, but between being haunted and infested, it felt entirely too crowded inside his own body, which was confused enough to begin with.

But the feeling of skin against his own was just so beguiling, so simple, so honest. He had lived most of his life starved of that contact and Drin, Drin had been a revelation. It was even worse, now that he was gone, to be...well, not quite alone. To be untouched.

Xeras rested his own hand over Carly's. "Not too many people put up with my presence, by choice. Let alone show an interest in making it a regular state of affairs."

"One thing I learned from Katinka's cats." Carly's hand inched down, pushing Xeras's leggings out of the way. "They get used to being stray. The wild puts a fear in them that makes them strike out at anyone who approached them. But it doesn't mean they want to be that way. It just means you have to be

91

patient."

Beneath the cover of their cloaks, Carly slid Xeras's hose down so they nestled together. Xeras felt Carly's cock pressing against him, Carly trying to pull away slightly. But Xeras eased his legs apart, leaning back so that the erect cock slid between his thighs up tight against his body.

"If you are under the impression I can be domesticated," Xeras said hoarsely. "You may yet be disappointed."

Carly's broad hand slid around, across Xeras's stomach. Xeras kept one arm wedged under his body to hide the dragon bump. That was rather going to limit things...but even that small movement pulled the blanket free from his knees letting the heat between them escape into the frigid night. Xeras cursed and pulled the cloaks around him again, all but wrenching them from Carly and precipitating an awkward tug of war.

Carly laughed. "If you ate a little better, you might not be so cold so much. You feel cool to the touch, you know. Like a corpse."

"How flattering," Xeras replied crossly. "Should I lie still and leave you to that little fantasy?"

But he reached back and felt Carly's muscular thigh and buttocks. It was a pleasing terrain, one he had to admit he hoped to get to know better. There was a slight stab of guilt, but he had Drin's blessing after all? He felt a slight warmth of confirmation, as if the troublesome ghost was not disregarding him entirely. He tried to ignore the potential audience to this awkward attempt at coupling.

"If you wish to stay entirely swaddled in this blanket," Carly said, "that will represent something of a limitation."

"I am sure you will manage if you care to."

And Carly did seem to be managing. His cock pressed in

between Xeras's thighs and slid up against the seam of his body with each small movement. Xeras's body's belated reaction kindled quickly. When Carly moved his hand down it provoked a wave of arousal that was almost unpleasantly intense. Xeras pressed back into Carly's welcoming embrace.

With closed eyes, Carly's touch was a revelation. He had only known one man's touch and Drin had never been so cautious. Perhaps Carly really did see him as some starved stray coming in from the cold.

Perhaps he was.

Carly stroked him up and down, teasingly slow and Xeras's flesh rose to fill his palm. Carly's warm breath brushed by his ear. Carly's hand and cock moved in concert and, between them, Xeras quickened, his skin warmed and he shivered at every touch, but it was no longer from the cold. Their bodies moved together so naturally, even confined within the taut covers folded over them. Although Carly laughed at how Xeras would stop every time the edge or corner got pulled up and make haste to fold it over again.

"You know it is a bit limiting if I'm not allowed to move here," he said.

Xeras tugged the blanket again, but Carly's end was pretty securely anchored under his substantial body.

"Well perhaps if I had woken up with you in my bed instead of the porcelain princess, we could have got off to a more comfortable start."

"Start?"

"You sound like the duchess now. That wasn't a proposal. Although I would propose that you stop laughing at me if you want to put *that* anywhere else tonight."

But Carly did not stop laughing. He held it in a little, but Xeras could feel his body shaking with it. "*That* is not what this is all about, but it seems to be a place you'll let me start and so I'll take it."

Carly reached down. With only spit to use, he seemed quite willing to take what was an offer. And precipitous as it might be, Xeras wanted it. He yearned for that feeling, of a man inside him, claiming and covering his body, the illusion that someone was there to protect him. That they would always be there.

He moaned as Carly pressed inside him, warming and opening, but fearing it all the same. They found a slow sweet rhythm that brought them both release. In the darkness afterward Xeras lay still. Carly's body warmed him though his own felt raw and strained, but sated. He tried not to think, he tried not to presume, he tried not to cry. And he did not give any further thought to the Bond of Hurn.

Chapter Nine

In the cold predawn Xeras awoke. Carly's body was still tight against his, legs and arms intertwined. Carly's arm and thigh looped over his in a way that seemed almost possessive, but certainly helped keep the chill at bay. He could tell Carly was awake from the way he moved, resting his chin against the back of Xeras's neck. There was a presumptuous familiarity in way he fitted Xeras into his embrace. Sure, they had done rather more than that last night, but most men understand that the imperatives of lust are not always an invitation to true intimacy. In the light of a new day, Xeras was uncertain.

Xeras feigned sleep a little longer, wondering what sort of man he had become. It was clear from Carly's advances, from the casual domesticity of his life, that he was not offering some passing comfort or making mercenary use of a warm body that happened to be nearby. In fact, rather the reverse. Xeras felt comfortable here, hard ground and perilous task aside, but searching his heart for feelings, he realized that he hardly knew Carly at all.

With a sigh, he pulled back his arm and leaned up on his elbow. "Seras? I have taken you at your word that you know how to deal with this dragon."

Indeed, the man did not know his correct name. That was Xeras's own fault, but fact was not affected by fault. It was simply what it was. "Certainly," Xeras replied. "There is an agreement in place that they should be observing. I need only remind them of this."

"They never struck me as particularly, um, rational creatures."

"They are quite rational, they just function by a somewhat different *rationale*." Xeras clutched the blankets to him.

"We still have a way to go today." Carly leaned down and placed a dry kiss on Xeras's cheek.

Xeras moved his legs tentatively. They seemed to creak in response; both knees refused to straighten, and one responded to the attempt with a surly, stabbing pain.

"You're a bit sore, no doubt," Carly said redundantly and not without ambiguity.

It was just as well the duke tried his luck early last night rather than after every one of Xeras's muscles had locked in place. At least it had stopped raining.

Do stop grumbling, darkling. You have—quite despite yourself—snagged a good one. Now turn around and leave Phinia's delightful parents to deal with their own oversized vermin.

Spurred on by what he recognized as his own contrariness, Xeras pushed himself into the sitting position. With his legs like logs and his butt having various reasons to complain, he wasn't quite sure how to get to his feet let alone proceed with their journey. Carly took this all in stride, getting up and heading over to the horses that stood hobbled, not too far away. Quite how a man grew up big, handsome and so even-tempered Xeras could not imagine.

Oh bloody hell, boy, you're actually suspicious that he is too nice? Well you're altogether too flighty these days and if Carly is offering to be an anchor, I suggest you grab hold and don't let go.

But what, exactly, would a man like that see in Xeras? In Tirrin he had the distinct advantage of being from one of the first families, the blood of Tirrin—wealthy and so on. Most people tolerated his prickly and self-absorbed manner and a few young ladies actually sought him out. Albeit only those whose families had a lot to gain by marrying into a higher status. Now what did he have to offer? Just a lack of any useful skills and a less-than-charming manner.

You could make some effort to do something about that. Unless you get some perverse satisfaction out of being miserable.

Xeras shrugged off that advice. Either Carly liked his men tall and contrary or the whole idea was doomed. He levered himself up awkwardly. Carly cast a look at him, but had better judgment than to offer assistance. Xeras realized one of the causes of his surly feelings.

Drin wasn't even slightly jealous.

⌈

Carly continued to quiz him as they rode on. Unwilling to admit the gaps and guesses in his knowledge, and not given the peace to try and unlock his stubborn memory, Xeras found himself bluffing.

"Yes, the yellow dragon will acknowledge the agreement. It and the peace it created has lapsed because it is specified as being in force only when humans remember and can cite it. And it does seem that the people of this region have forgotten the Bond of Hurn."

"And you haven't."

"And I haven't."

"Being from Tirrin, as you are."

Xeras remained silent, not willing to concede any connection to a world he was desperate to leave behind. His body slowly relaxed into the swaying body of the horse beneath him. The land was higher, but more bare and level, allowing them to ride side by side as they ascended the shoulder of the mountainside. His stolid steed picked its footing with due care and he came to put his trust in it, him—Lefty—entirely. He ventured a quick pat to Lefty's shoulder. Belatedly, he noticed the growing silence was not entirely unstrained and turned to see Carly watching him intently.

"So what *is* a Ballot Duke, then?" Xeras said, hoping to deflect his attention.

Carly's tilted brow suggested the ploy was transparent, but he obliged. "The Duchy of Ballot's Keep is little more than the town itself and a wide but wild tract of land that stretches from a small parcel of arable land below to the arid table. The town controls the only negotiable pass between the two. That small dominion, along with the ancient gate, allows us to require a toll for those passing through—and for many, many years a hereditary tyranny ruled over the area. A remnant left behind with the withdrawal of the Tirrinian overlords in the early stages of the wars. The men who had colluded with that rule managed to perpetuate their own awhile."

"But that all changed," Xeras said, not without skepticism. Every rule tended to paint the past in a negative light to aggrandize its own position.

"Several generations before this time, while farther inland Tirrin fought to hold its conquests, we had our own uprising. And in its aftermath, the people felt a great desire to avoid ever delivering the town and its assets into the hands of another royal dynasty. So it was determined that a duke would be chosen by lot from all adult men of the town and he would in turn choose a woman to be the lady of the office. Generally a spouse, but in my case, my good sister. And that with his demise or voluntary retirement, the procedure would be repeated so the title never became inherited. I am the seventh Ballot Duke to be raised to that office."

Xeras frowned as he pondered that peculiar form of government. It seemed inherently unstable in that men, as they age, naturally want to secure power for their heirs. And yet in this town, this fate seemed to have been avoided on six prior occasions. There must be more to this method than was encompassed in Carly's simplistic description, and quite possibly more than an honest man such as he was aware of.

Together they crested the bow of the rocky summit and before them lay the bowl of a small, shallow, hidden valley nestled in the crux of several mountain peaks. It was surrounded on all other sides by jagged summits that rose up precipitously to a long range stretched out to both sides. From this vantage, Xeras could appreciate how the land here dropped steeply behind them back towards Ballot's Keep, with only one break where a more gradual path could be discerned from the tablelands to the lowlands that undulated down towards the distant sea. It was easy to see the one easily navigable path from the arid lands or the horse tribes to the lowlands was spanned by the narrow filament of the town's enormous gate, which effectively blocked one great expanse of land from another.

How did such an immense structure come to be? He wondered. For it was surely beyond the ability of one small town to construct. Perhaps a legacy left by Tirrin, from the days of empire when labor could be conscripted from many lands to do as the conclave willed. Perhaps the work of Tirrin mages or those from an earlier time.

The small valley before them was for the most part barren, its gentle contours a result of grey rubble and sand, not soil or vegetation.

Carly gathered his reins. "We should not stay out in the open."

Xeras could see a large cave in the far valley side, surrounded by rock that seemed torn and broken; the sharp edges glinted in the midmorning light.

"I think you should go no farther than this," Xeras said.

Good idea. Somebody should be left alive to bury whatever parts of you the dragon spits out.

"You can see me from here," Xeras said. He nudged Lefty forward. The horse took a few steps then craned his thick neck back to where Carly waited. "Don't worry," Xeras assured Carly and horse alike with as much confidence as he could feign. "The dragon will be more likely to listen to me if I go alone." And he pressed on.

Oh brilliant. Snag a nice, wealthy young man, and leave him behind to walk into a dragon's den. If a more foolish action can possibly be conceived of, it is beyond the grasp of my imagination.

"He'd be no used to me once he'd been through the gut and gullet of a dragon, anyway," Xeras replied blithely.

Is that a good reason to precede him?

Xeras laughed. He had a heady, source-less feeling of confidence as he rode onwards. The Bond of Hurn, that was the key. If there weren't so many interruptions, it would be clearer in his mind. He traversed the barren bowl of the small valley in a calm fugue, set on his course. Xeras dared not even turned and look back. It would not take much to provoke Carly to follow him.

"Sir Dragon," he called out in the beast's own tongue as he drew close. "Or is it madam?"

There was an inelegant snort from ahead of him and a warm gust blew from the mouth of the cave, carrying with it the stench of effluence and carrion. A grinding, dragging sound presaged the emergence of the beast itself, somewhat larger than Plegura with a great pallid head like an upturned boat. Its eyes fixed on him blearily.

"Dragon," Xeras said firmly. "I have come to remind you of the Bond of Hurn by which the dragons promise not to harry or harass peoples under the sway of a lord of the land, or their beasts or their domiciles. The agreement abides so long as there lives one of each race who remembers and honors what each has promised. The dragons are to direct their depredations only to the animals of the wood and stream. The men to offer up those willing and able...oh yes, that was it, wasn't it..."

Lefty, being a sensible beast, didn't wait for him to rein up, but stopped of his own accord some distance back from the cave.

"I thought it was a mistranslation," Xeras addressed the dragon. "But what it said was something to the effect that the man had to offer up to the dragon one capable of bearing and carrying for their young. Now I do believe most scholars interpreted that to mean a damsel or virgin of some sort. Although quite what a dragon would actually want with a damsel I do not know, unless their meat is more tend...uh!"

Lefty made a last-minute attempt at flight, but the dragon surged out from its lair and reached forward with a darting grab. Its great paw wrapped around horse and rider both, thrusting Xeras forward in his saddle and squeezing his chest so that he could not take a breath. He heard the horse squeal in terror and felt it struggling beneath him, crushed against him by the dragon's grasp so that Xeras was sure this would be the ignominious manner of his death.

Chapter Ten

Xeras didn't really want to wake up. Even in a cloudy semiawareness, he could tell one thing about the reality he would emerge into, it was going to be cold. And so, by an act of will, he hovered in the margins between the dark depth of oblivion and the uncertain charms of awareness.

But you are going to get bored of this fairly soon. Always had an active mind, darkling. Always needed something to think about. Stimulation as grist to the mill.

And Drin's endless blathering as grist to that same mill, or perhaps just grit in the machinery.

Well, charming. But it's well time you woke up. Things to be doing...

Which was a mildly interesting proposition. After being snatched up by a dragon, what exactly would he have to wake up and do, be digested? Logically he wasn't being digested, that would probably be warm.

Damn it, now he *was* awake.

Xeras opened his eyes, and was struck with dazzling light that made him close them immediately. As an opening gambit, that was something of a mistake. He curled his fingers. The grimy ground scratched under his knuckles let him know he lay on his back. His fingers were numb and gusting wind blew over his chest where his rucked-up tunic exposed his stomach, the torn hem fluttering against his skin. There was a quality to the sound of the wind, an open emptiness, that worried him.

Groping to the sides, he felt uneven stone around him. With an exasperated sigh, he rolled on his side and raised one hand to shield his eyes, opening them more cautiously. He glimpsed the natural stone beneath him, and slowly cupped his hand upwards, peering through the glare. The rocky ground meandered gradually down and terminated suddenly. The cloudy expanse beyond suggested an unpleasant reason for that.

Looking around he saw a plateau that extended back a way, maybe thirty paces, then jutted upwards. There was one strange lumpy object in between. He fixed his eyes upon it, but couldn't discern what it was.

Curiosity, always with the curiosity.

Xeras pulled his tunic down. With the wind and the way the ground canted towards what seemed to be a cliff, he didn't dare stand—even though the edge was some distance off. He got on hands and knees. The hard stone was sharp and uneven, pressing into his skin. He moved forward slowly, stiffly.

Even before he got to the lump, his hand fell on a desiccated tatter of skin. The remnant of tawny hair was stained pink with blood.

It was Lefty. Or it had been.

Xeras kept on crawling past, trying not to look at it. He couldn't help but see what remained—the bare ribcage pointing upwards, the leg jutting stiffly into the air. He skirted around it and got to the protruding rock. It pushed up about the height of two men. He finally stood, clinging to it. He shuffled along the outcropping to get the carcass out of sight. Then seeing a path he climbed carefully, high enough to really get an idea of where he was.

The great, flat-topped rock thrust out of wooded land that extended to the horizon in all directions. It was the largest of a series of buttresses that loomed, high above the canopy. The wind buffeted him as if determined to pitch him over the cliff to the verdant land below. He needed to find shelter. But he also needed to get out of here before the dragon returned for desert.

Forgive me for saying this but...

"You told me so. That must be one thing you and my father agree on. I could never be told anything."

I don't recall Harus offering you a great deal of counsel. But we are running into some obstacles where trial and error does not seem like a sensible approach. There are only so many errors of this magnitude you are going to survive.

Nor, Xeras considered, was it a given he would survive this one.

Xeras had always hated heights. He didn't even like to look out of the windows of Tirrin's famed towers. So he timorously came to appreciate the full extent of his new domain. The entire area was no more than one hundred paces from end to end. It rose slightly in the centre but offered no cave or cover. Yellowed bones and grisly remains suggested that the dragon brought its prey here to consume in a place of security, or store against a time of need. The sides were sheer and fell away a dizzying distance to the forest floor. Far too far to fall and survive.

The best shelter he could find was in the leeside of the wind, hunched down with his back against the low central outcropping, but the buffeting winds curled around and found him. He felt tears in his eyes and although he could blame it on the wind, on fear, on many things, it was actually for that damn horse. Or maybe the horse was an excuse his mind had fixed upon. Why would that beast mean anything to him, especially now, when his own life was in immediate danger?

But he'd got to like Lefty. That horse had a lot of patience; he was simply what he was, a useful and amiable animal. And, more importantly, Xeras had gotten him killed. He was proving adept at doing that to anyone, *thing,* whatever, that he cared for. He huddled down with his arms crossed over his chest and knees drawn up tight and felt the tears and general misery force their way out of his body in bubbling, foolish coughs.

Finally he ventured over to the horse's remains, haphazardly strewn about and noticeably incomplete. The saddle was missing, the blanket was still rolled up neatly. It was pinned under a ragged remnant of horseflesh that was blackening where the torn edges were exposed to the air. He tugged it out gingerly. One end was rent by sharp claws. Blood and gore stained most of the rest. Still he needed it. He retreated, wrapping the blanket around him with a grimace, and crouched in the shallow depression and lee slope that was the closest thing to shelter he could find.

He waited for some kind of thought to come to him. Drin was right about one thing, his was usually a busy mind. In the long blank moment that followed, his mind responded with little more than a hostile shrug. Apparently it was better at getting him into trouble than out.

Give yourself a little time, darkling.

"How much time do I have, Drin? That dragon may be back anytime."

You can't fly away from here. What else can you do?

"Freeze, or fall," Xeras replied sharply. "And that being the case, a quicker death may be preferable to a slow and uncomfortable one."

Don't you say that sort of thing to me! You wanted to speak to the dragon? Then hang around to try and do just that.

Xeras was quiet a while. He felt Drin's regard. The wraith

was clearly saying whatever he thought would convince Xeras. Drin hadn't wanted him to talk to the dragon in the first place and experience hadn't supported the wisdom of the strategy. Xeras also found himself thinking of Carly. The duke must have seen him carried off, helpless to do anything, probably fearing he was dead already. Strange there should be two people who cared about his fate, albeit one of them dead and the other barely met. Time he took a little more interest in the matter himself.

"I'm not going to do anything stupid," he reassured the ghost.

That'll be a nice change.

Xeras's twist of irritation was muted. This wasn't something he could deny. But now he *was* stuck with the plan he had fixed on from the outset. He had to hope that the yellow dragon would come back and listen to him. The Bond of Hurn. It was a real pact; it still meant something. And he had to think of a back-up plan against failure. Forced to depend on his own resources, he found them rather meager. Xeras experienced a moment of desolate self-doubt that perfectly matched the scene around him.

I wish I could hold you now. I wish I could touch you.

"I don't know that you should be here with me, Drin. I think you have somewhere else that you are meant to be. Because I wish I could touch you too." With a wry smile he recalled, "You were always so warm, like you had a fever. It used to drive me crazy the way you would hold me so tight. It was like trying to sleep on a hearthstone."

A long silence stretched out. He could feel Drin's nearness, like a shadow falling over him. These days his presence, no matter how familiar and how beloved, felt cold. And although Xeras was not the mage his blood should have made him, he had come to face the fact that Drin was here, and that he should not be. The late awakening of his gift should make that a matter at least partially under his control. If he did not want to be haunted he should do something about it.

"Maybe it is time we both let go."

Drin didn't reply. Xeras hugged the blood-stiffened blanket to him, but the cold sank deeper into his muscles and bones. He stood suddenly and shuffled closer, considering the void. He felt Drin's alarm.

"I am just looking. Is there not some chink or path..."

It is a sheer drop, darkling. Do not venture it. Please, this once, do listen to me.

There was not much else to do for the next little while but listen. His head ached, he was too uncomfortable to rest, and too frightened. He sometimes paced, feeling the numbing cold in his feet; sometimes he huddled, curled up tight. As it grew dark, his eyes were drawn to a movement in the sky. He stood, peering into the bitter wind that drew new tears to his eyes. The dark flicker grew steadier, larger, closer. The dragon was returning.

He stepped forward, eyes fixed on the beast as it circled heavily over the rocky island. Its wings, stretched out taut against the wind, cast a wide shadow. He could even hear the slight scraping sound of the scales of its hide shifting with each movement. The dragon's size overhead was daunting.

"You must release me," Xeras called against the wind. "I demand that you observe the terms of the Bond of Hurn. It is my right!" He knew the truth of it, as he said it. He felt the conviction.

His hand fell to his side. His skin was frozen and tight and he wondered how the little parasite was doing. It might be the crux of the whole matter. It sprang to his mind now: the Bond of Hurn by which the dragons promise not to harass...or the beast of their domiciles...so long as there lives one of each race...who remembers and reveres what mages and dragons share...that magic comes to men as continuance to the serpent race...power to one, through *get* to the other.

It had meant very little to him at the time. Words learned by rote to gain mastery in an obscure, near-extinct but complex tongue. He spoke it now, bluntly. He finally understood, at least a little. He grasped the frayed edge of the tapestry too old, too faded and too degraded to be viewed clearly. He understood "get" in this case meant offspring. The dragon needed, for some reason, human assistance in their breeding. What he did not quite understand was the issue of magic. *Magic comes to men...*

"I carry one of your race," Xeras shouted upwards at the great dragon that held its position over the outcropping, gliding in the wind. "I honor the bond. I demand..."

A loud reverberating thud made him leap aside and fall. Something landed with a resounding thud and rebounded. The jumbled, torn, but entire carcass of some kind of sheep or goat covered in a thick shaggy coat. He could see the yellow dragon drawing up its clawed paws, tight to its body after dropping its...what? Missile? Offering?

It stayed positioned overhead, straining like sails tacking into the wind, membranes shuddering. Xeras cowered, fearing that he might be snatched up. But what was his other option, to stay on this exposed rock until he was forced to face the choice he had so glibly offered Drin? He stood up straight.

"You must release me. If I die, so does the young one!"

He could not even tell if his words reached the dragon against the screeching of the wind. A deep rumble rolled over the stone. At first he took it to be thunder, presaging conditions would soon become even less hospitable. But then he heard the syllables, drawn out like the bellow of a stag trying to speak like a man. The sound was coming from the dragon.

"I...provide," the dragon said in a crackling moan that seemed to take minutes. And with a dip of its wing, it slid to the side and slipped away on the winds. Soon it was so distant that it would obviously be futile to attempt to speak further. Finally, all he could see was mist and cloud.

"Another brilliant conversationalist," Xeras muttered. "I did better with Plegura."

You did altogether too well with Plegura. But why is this one bringing you dead animals?

"If I were a dragon, this would be everything I need. Up away from any threat." He indicated the sheep with one rigid finger. "Well fed and cared for. This yellow dragon is presumptuous and clearly not too bright, but actually trying to look after me. Or at least protect the get. It could certainly have killed me before now, if that was its intent."

It brought to mind his father's many late night lectures. One of the more common themes was that Xeras would never last long outside the safety and succor of his father's house. All evidence to the contrary, he refused to let the bastard be right. With new resolve, Xeras looked around the scant resources he had been offered. He was getting the hell off this rock.

☙

Talk to me, Xeras.

Days had passed with the yellow dragon passing overhead now and again, but never so much as touching the surface of the outcropping. Its discourse was limited, but Xeras came to understand that it was indeed motivated out of some misguided desire to protect the dragon get he carried. The lump on his side seemed larger but he could not really tell. A diet of raw meat was winnowing away the meager reserves his body retained. It might simply be that the surrounding tissue was becoming less ample.

It would be charitable to describe Xeras's new overgarment as an uncured fleece. The raw hide still bore remnants of meat and the air heaved with moisture that prevented it from drying. Still it provided some barrier against the cold.

Xeras?

"Yes, Drin. I am here. Leaving aside the question of where I could possibly have gone. I could hardly have exited in a way that failed to take you with me."

Twisting in his hands were slippery strips of hide, laboriously cut with a shard of rock. He braided them tightly together in the hope it would make them strong enough to bear his weight. The gnarled, knotted mess was the work of four days and still only five arms' length. Nor was he sure what he would tie it to on this largely featureless terrain.

He sighed and flung it down, not for the first time. "Sorry." He stared out into the cloudy void. "What did you ever see in me anyway?" he asked Drin, knowing his exasperation was guiding his words, but unable stop it. He had, in the back of his mind, always wondered. "Other than a status I was born into, the wealth I would have inherited, what possible reason would there be?"

You asked me that before, do you remember?

"You said I was beautiful, which I am not. And that I was intelligent when I am merely well educated."

Which was only the first two of my reasons, but there was no answer I could give you that you would accept. Has that changed?

"Will you not humor me, and try again?"

Why do you ask now, of all times?

Xeras sighed and picked up the makeshift rope again. Finding one of the three strands coming to an end, he set to the tricky task of tying on the next length with enough of a loose end to pull tight without slipping free. The rancid smell of spoiling animal fat made him grimace. Like there was much to do on this rock but make feeble escape plans, and talk.

"I was wondering about Carly," he confessed. "I am now a person entirely without station, and I was not even marginally courteous to him. Do you really think...well, that night we, Carly and I, were *together*, and you were pretending not to pay any attention..."

His thoughts and fingers stilled.

"Drin, do you truly think he...liked me? Do you really not mind?"

Drin's laugh was warm and light, just as he remembered it. *The first time we lay together, I told you that I did not think humans were meant to have just one mate, and you tensed up like the rabbit under the eyes of a hawk. So I let it drop. I realize some people are like that. And maybe after a while I was, too. But even if I were the jealous type, I am beyond that now. My goal is not to stay with you. It is to know that it is safe to leave you.*

"I don't want you to leave me." And that was true for all that it seemed wrong to hold Drin back from wherever he was meant to go. For all that he had spent long months sure that Drin's voice was just a facet of his growing madness and wanting it to go away. Maybe now he was embracing the madness. It had a certain familiarity. It was a comfort. The last comfort he had left and a lifeline of a kind.

I'll never leave you, whether you can hear me or not. Not

until you bid me to go.

And in the mists that wended over the surface of the rock, Xeras saw a twist, a wisp, a form slowly, softly growing. Then Drin was there, standing before him, an apparition with a smile. He had never seen Drin's ghost before—if this was deeper madness he welcomed it. Drin's lips move as he spoke. His beloved face, so ordinary and so piercingly real.

I loved your serious nature, Xeras. I even loved your sadness because I could make you smile, and no one else could. That fed my vanity, I confess. There was a secret Xeras you showed only to me.

I loved how you always noticed me, so acutely, even when it began to give us away. I loved how every word or touch was a revelation to you like you were some creature lifted out of its shell into the bright, sharp daylight. I loved how you loved me, although at the end I feared it was too much, that you clung to me too tightly because your life had offered you so little else— rather than because you wanted me. That wounded my vanity, but I needed that as much as anything.

And I feared what would happened if you were ever left behind, alone. I loved you for all these reasons. And if Carly loves you, which I think he does, or could, it will be for his own reasons and not for mine. And if you love him, or could, which I think you could, you need to finish that rope.

༄

Snow began to fall steadily and Xeras lost track of the days of his isolation. It probably had not been that many, but his mind was not exactly sharp. He should have marked them off somehow, with pebbles or scratches on the rock.

The rope was coiled, gnarled and uneven as his feet. No way of knowing if it would be long enough, but it would get no longer. There wasn't a scrap left to use. He had even sacrificed the greater part of his clothing, the tops of his boot, the fleece he'd used as a coat. He'd cut the strands finer as he went so the whole length narrowed like a whip towards the end.

To the bottom end he tied the old blanket as a weight and marker. The top was wound around a rock that he wedged in a crevice.

If you wait, the dragon may fetch us some new kill.

"It has been three days since we last saw it. We cannot be sure it will return. These dragons do seem, no pun intended, a flighty lot."

He ran the length of the plaited rope through his hand feeling every uncertain knot, slippery and makeshift. Drin's insubstantial presence floated at his shoulder. He had been visually perceptible on and off for days, although often as little more than a blur. It had been a comfort to see Drin again, even so vaguely.

"Thank you, Drin. For everything."

A lot of use I've been. There should be some kind of training for this stuff. A guidebook for ghosts and guardian spirits...

Xeras shook his head, kicking the blanket over the edge. The rope pulled taut and squeaked protest, even at carrying that weight, but it held. He could not see whether it reached the ground. The stony protrusion he was on bulged at the top, like a mushroom. The rope swayed beneath him, swinging in and out of sight. It looked like the blanket did not reach the tops of the trees, but it was close, close enough. It would have to be.

Fear ran through him, making his arms weak, his hands shake. He wiped wet palms on his equally wet leggings, mainly to delay the moment where he would have to begin his descent.

"Nothing for it now," Xeras muttered. "I'm sorry, Drin, for getting you killed. Perhaps I'll be with you soon." He felt guilty, knowing Drin didn't like such defeatist talk. But for once Drin let it go lightly.

Don't hurry on my account.

Despite having announced his intentions, it took a good while to get his courage in hand and make a start. Xeras lay flat on the stone, on his stomach, and swung his legs out into the void. Even with Drin so constant by his side, there was another image in his mind: Carly, and Ballot's Keep. He couldn't deny it now; he was far too terrified to prevaricate. He wasn't sure what he wanted there, and whether it would really want him back once they were properly acquainted. He had a goal, something to live for other than what the busybody dragons had in mind.

His fingers gripped tight, white-skinned and frozen numb as he lowered himself. Sheer panic brought tears to his eyes as he dangled over the edge on a slender strand that creaked and swayed. His hand slipped, the rope sliding through his fingers as he cursed and struggled to hold on. He made his way down mainly by clutching as tight as his fear-weakened limbs would allow and sliding gradually downwards despite it all. Eventually he felt he couldn't hold on any longer. Something slapped against his foot; the blanket tied to the very end of the rope. Peering down, he could see that the tips of the treetops were still a dizzying distance below him. The perspective had fooled him, or his own desperate hopes. He strove with all his will to keep a grip, but slid down until he clung to the blanket itself knotted to the end, swaying and twisting in the wind. The stone cliff face was far beyond reach, sheer and vertical and even if the rope would hold as he swung towards it, he would find nothing to hold on to there. He started to sway wider and twist in the teeth of the wind and the sinews of the rope groaned.

He didn't have the strength in his frigid arms to climb back up. And yet his fear was too great, he could not let go and hope to grab something to break his fall. He swung and turned. He saw Drin again, floating in the air before him. Seeing his pensive face really didn't help, but at least he wasn't being subject to the usual commentary on his actions. Although, now that he thought about it, it would be nice to hear Drin's voice, one last time.

He opened his mouth to comment that he would have little time left to regret when, with a wrenching snap and jerk, the rope gave way. He plummeted down, flailing out with his arms. Drin's anguished face receded rapidly from him, and Xeras saw Drin reaching towards him. He could have sworn the wraith's hands clutched his tunic and slowed his fall for one brief moment. In a bright flash, Drin was gone and the air rushed up like a great wind from below. Except he knew in a last moment of fatalism that it was quite the reverse.

Then the tree branches slapped at him. A bough hit him hard at the small of his back and he somersaulted, tumbling and rebounding. He hit the ground facedown, hard. So hard his body bounced back up. He lost track of things awhile. Things like his name, where he was and why he was in so much pain.

Chapter Eleven

The pain in his side was not so much intense as grotesquely wrong. Xeras was sure he would peer down and find some splintered branch speared right through him. He pieced together what had happened and was profoundly surprised that he was still alive. He didn't want to look and see what state he was in.

But there was a sound, a creaking crashing sound like one of those trees might fall on top of him. Which might be a fast way out, rather than the slow crippled-and-bleeding-to-death state of affairs. Causes of death were starting to queue up and he was not up to running away from them anymore. But an annoying little thing changed inside Xeras right at the most inconvenient moment.

He actually wanted to live.

It was enough to make him believe in those prating Gods his father always went on about. Any Gods the old man doted on would be perverse sorts. The kind that waited around until a man found something to live for and then throw every nasty murderous circumstance they could at him.

But, to cut a long story short, he did want to live and so he must make a token effort on his own behalf. Opening his eyes— well, one of them, the other seemed uncooperative—he saw his own more-or-less-intact, but undeniably battered body and, beyond it, pale shards of broken timber poking up through the ferns and underbrush. The scene was confusing, because in the sudden convergence between him and the trees, it could not have been the trees that had broken.

All become clear when a large yellow paw settled over the debris, the claws scoring the exposed wood. The yellow dragon. Gods be damned. He had gone to these lengths, put Drin through a terrible scare and in all probability killed himself. Everything he had done, all for nothing. Xeras closed his eyes and pressed his face into the ground. The Gods laugh at men's plans.

Ah, nice ground, soft, fragrant...soft. He was so frustrated he could scream, but something would probably shake loose if he tried. Just out of principle he would try his best to run away. He wasn't looking forward to that. He started a countdown as motivation. Three, two...

There was another, louder thud just to the side of him. Looking again, he saw a solid rocky pillar about as wide as the largest tree in the forest, the one that would take three or four men hand in hand to ring around. The illusion fooled him at first, but he realized quickly what it was. The stone dragon. He hoped this was good news. If there was any dragon who might be counted as his ally it was this one. He felt a peculiar surge of relief at seeing the big grey dragon.

Funny how quickly his feelings had shifted on that. Xeras experienced a moment's suspicion about how the little dragon-tadpole thing was affecting him. *Here comes daddy, eh? Just because you are pleased, doesn't mean I have to be. Although we are something of a package deal right now.*

The yellow dragon backed off, toppling huge trees in its wake. Xeras had to turn his head and peer over his aching nose to see the stone dragon's leg on the other side of him, its looming body directly overhead.

"Do not move," the stone dragon said. Unlike the yellow dragon, his voice was almost human in its pitch and volume. It had never occurred to Xeras just how incongruous that was given the creature's form. "If you have killed the infant, you will have more to fear from me than you ever did from Ghardis. Stay still and we will have the greatest chance of ensuring you and the infant survive."

That should have frightened him, and yet it didn't really. He stayed dutifully still, all the same. The stone dragon lumbered over him, about as carefully as anything that size could. The two dragons were partly concealed by the remnants of the vegetation. The stone dragon's voice was too quiet to hear from that distance and the other one, *Ghardis?*, had a rumbling tone that was hard to. make out at the best of times. Their conversation was not amicable. Ghardis finally gave out a roar like waves, but a thousand times louder. His head and long straight neck emerged against the sky as he reared up. The dragon's face didn't show expression, but every line of his body was belligerent and his thick tail hit another swathe of timber like a giant battering ram. There was going to be some kind of fight, something that wouldn't be easily contained and Xeras was the prize, or the get he carried.

Xeras rolled onto his side. Nothing pinned him down, but one of his arms was obviously broken and he couldn't breathe through his nose. It didn't seem terribly plausible that he was alive, let alone capable of movement. He felt a twinge of doubt about moving. The stone dragon had told him to stay put. Yet that impulse of obedience seemed not quite to be his own. He had never known himself to be biddable—quite perversely the reverse, in fact.

If he was going to be contrary he should at least be consistent about it. Very carefully he leaned onto the elbow of his arm that seemed more or less entire. He wanted to see what the dragon get looked like. But his other arm—he felt a little queasy just looking at it—was clearly in no shape to reach down and lift his tunic.

And he had to do something. What was it? It was hard to keep his thoughts from floating off to the tune of the buzzing in his head. A resounding thud helped him focus on the immediate peril. Glancing over, he saw the two dragons collide like rams in mating season. Locked together, they swayed towards him. The stone dragon so four-square and solid, but Ghardis much taller, his long hind legs braced and digging deep into the ground. If there was a fate worse than having a building fall on you, or falling off a cliff, it would probably be getting trampled by warring dragons. Xeras wasn't inclined to find out.

He didn't try to stand up, but pulled himself along, seeking the cover of the cliff he had just so precipitously descended. He pushed himself to sit with his back to the rock. The pain seemed to dull, but other sensations were going with it. His vision was foggy and his skin numb. He did finally lift his tunic and saw the whole of his torso ribboned with twisted scarlet bruises and vivid purple contusions.

It was an instinct to brace for Drin's scolding and when it didn't come he had to fill the void.

"That was very stupid," Xeras instructed himself patiently. "This really isn't good."

"Really, how could you tell?" he replied. "I have always assumed that lacerations and protruding bones were a good sign, a natural side effect of normal boyish enthusiasm."

Xeras got the feeling the fall had shaken something loose in his head as well. Surveying the damage with detached dismay, he also saw that the dragon bump was squashed and

119

discolored; the edge of it was ruptured and sluggishly leaking a thick, translucent fluid. That sight, more than any other, caused real alarm to constrict his chest. Not just for what was happening to him. But the little one, too. As a father of dragons, he had been remiss in his duties in every possible way.

"That is not good," Xeras repeated.

He missed Drin. It didn't seem fair that he was going to die here, or that the dragon bump was going with him before it even had a chance to live. One of Xeras's eyes was sealed shut. Under his fumbling fingers, the whole area felt disconcertingly squishy, but his eye was probably still intact as far as he could tell. Squinting with the other, he saw the dragons circling. They stood, each pushing against the other's flank so they circled around, butting and biting at the other's body. It went on and on, a fight to be determined more by stamina than strength.

Ghardis's tail swishing out behind him. Stubby wings flared up from the stone dragon's back, more like two spiny crests that jutted from his shoulders and tapered down his back. Stubby in relation to his body, that is. Either one would have cover the roof of a substantial house and left a little over for an awning.

The two dragons slowed, pressing against each other but not moving, straining and panting. They circled back the other way. The stone dragon strove forward, barely making any progress at first, but then forcing his opponent back faster and faster.

"Drin?" Xeras tried again. "I could really use one of your smart-ass comments just about now."

No reply. He couldn't help think of that flash as Drin vanished, of the feeling that—just for a moment—the ghost's grasp had slowed his descent. What if Drin was somehow gone, finally really gone?

The dragons spiraled, moving farther away until the crashing and thudding and shaking of the ground was the only evidence of their continued combat. Xeras felt a sinister tickling sensation inside his body and a shortness of breath. Regardless of which of the creatures triumphed, they might soon have cause to be disappointed by what they won. Presumably no matter how the dragon bump fared, it would be incapable of drawing sustenance from a corpse.

He slumped sideways down the rock, but could not find the strength to right himself as his one good eye slipped closed.

Chapter Twelve

Not many men would immediately recognize the sensation of being carried in the paw of a dragon. Albeit a broader and steadier hand than the one he last knew.

"Do not stir," the stone dragon said. "We are almost there."

"Almost wh—"

The dragon opened his digits and looked down with an implacable expression. "I said do not stir."

The movement exposed a view of shrubbery broken by the trunks of towering trees. Ambling down a slope, the dragon drew to a stop.

"Marlha," the dragon called. "I have a boon to ask of you."

Xeras lay on his back, feeling his clothes stuck to his body. His arm lying over his chest still showed exposed bone. The dragon lowered its great hand-like paw and tilted its palm. Xeras's protest came out as an inarticulate shriek and he rolled over to land on some kind of planked surface.

"This is the one?" said a cracked female voice from nearby. "Is the get still alive?"

"As yet," the dragon replied. "But it has been harmed. Do what you can."

A loud stumping sound suggested that was as much as he had to say on the matter. Xeras remained face down. His broken arm sprawled out to the side and felt excruciatingly wrong. But that injury was a boon to the extent that it drowned out all of the other aches and pains to the point that he could not itemize them.

"I'm an old lady," the voice said. "If you are coming inside, it's going to have to be under your own power."

Xeras's attempt at a reply was little more than a dry mumble, but with a surge of irritation he tried again. "I *mill* thtay where I am, thank you."

A hefty foot pressed against his side and propelled him onto his back, causing his arm to drag over the ground. Too many curse words flashed through his head. They tangled together and none made it out of his mouth.

"Up to you," she said. "But it's going to be a cold night."

Xeras could see only a vague outline of a figure standing over him. He distinctly heard each step as she went inside what was presumably her dwelling, then after a long spell returned, stooping with an irritated sigh. She rifled through his clothing, locating the dragon bump and prodding it carefully, wielding what felt like a damp cloth or rag.

Xeras was inclined to suggest that she might look at his arm. But likely her priorities were rather different from his. He did hope the little one would somehow survive. Strange how quickly his feelings had changed. But his feelings were not entirely his own of late, as the dragon bump was exerting some insidious influence over his mind. All the same, he did care. So he lay still.

In due course she turned her attentions to the rest of his body. "What you need to do is this. You are clearly in no shape to look after yourself for very long in the wild forest that extends for a good stretch in every direction from here. Therefore it would behoove you to do as I ask. The egg's sac has been ruptured beyond the point that it can be healed, but the dragon get lives and the umbilicus is intact. Are you listening?"

She poked her finger sharply into the only substantial expanse of intact skin he had left, just over his left armpit.

"Mmm," he replied.

"Focus your will on giving the get the power to breathe. Focus your will on it breathing air and its skin toughening to keep in blood and fluids. Focus on that. For if the get dies before you equip it for life outside the sac, I will bury you both in the same grave."

So she was strong enough to dig graves, but not to move injured men. Xeras supposed it was largely a matter of motivation. He gave himself a long wordless moment to despair and then accepted the reality of his situation. The get was like a bird developing in an egg. The shell had cracked and it needed to grow up fast.

"Not up," the woman contradicted. "You must not have it waste energy on increasing in size. It has very limited resources and need be no bigger to exist independently. This would not naturally occur for some months or even years but it should be possible. Think of its breath and its skin. Think hard and do not doubt that I will know if you are complying."

Oh good. The spooky old woman could read his thoughts. He paused to see if she was going to give him any further confirmation and was rewarded with nothing more than silence.

Xeras kept his mind as blank as possible. He knew nothing about this woman and she didn't need to know anymore about him. The only question right now was how to get some assistance from her, and so he needed to do what she said.

He felt a habitual kick of rebellion at the idea of being coerced into compliance. But his insides conspired with his environment. Gods be damned, but he did want the little parasite to live. And besides, if it could breathe and be out in the air, he could get rid of it. He could get the dragon bump off without doing it any harm.

So while his instinct was to rail against the woman leaving him wounded, probably dying, here on the dusty porch, Xeras instead did what she asked. He only missed Drin's warm voice advising him.

Not really knowing how to proceed, he merely focused on his own breathing. Each intake provoked a dull pain, but his lungs obligingly filled and emptied.

This is what you are going to need, little monster.

He tried clumsily to will an ability, the very structure of breath, into the dragon get's body. He thought of the way he heard Drin's voice without there being any real sound. It was an idea sent between them. Now he had some thoughts to send to the get.

"You should give it a name," the woman said. He was startled to hear her so nearby, kneeling beside him again. "You keep on encouraging it to breathe; it'll take your mind off this."

She pulled his arm straight. With a bellow Xeras jerked upright. The woman slammed him back down hard, a hand to his chest. His head rebounded off the boards.

"Mind the get," she snapped.

Xeras clamped his jaw shut. Waves of cool nausea washed over him. Mind the get indeed. If wishing could make it so, the get was going to grow into a towering monster that would swoop down in this benighted place one of these days and use this old lady for a toothpick.

Get ready to start breathing little one; I have a job for you.

He felt his mangled arm grabbed again...

☙

He came to in the cool of the evening. A musty quilt lay haphazardly over him, leaving his feet dangling in the cold air.

Breathing yet? he asked the get, not entirely convinced his will had any impact on whatever the little thing was up to.

Drin?

Still no response there. He lay still, feeling altogether sorry for himself as he listened vaguely to the ticking, piping call of some bird in the shrubbery. He could only hope this part of the world didn't support too much in the way of large predatory animals like wolves or bears, because he was pretty much the buffet as he was—already fully tenderized and partly filleted.

Peering to the left, he saw his left arm was straighter and swaddled tight onto a wooden plank that lay flat on the floor. That looked like a good idea. Having satisfied himself on that account, his body felt free to notify him of its other grievances. His head thudded, his mouth was parched and his whole body ached from inside to out. His left eye was still swollen over in a pouch of inflamed flesh. But running a small inventory, he found the rest of his body parts were present and moved tentatively, if with protest, when he asked it of them. Although more than an almost imperceptibly small degree of motion seemed inadvisable.

As he contemplated the mixed blessing of his short-term survival, the dragon get squirmed against his side. It was not just a movement under his skin, but deeper. A thread ran from the creature right into his guts.

Breathing, he remembered, and skin. *Get on with it, little thing. Breathe in, breathe out, get tough and ready for life on the outside, because the free ride is over. I've got enough to deal with here myself. Time for you to go.*

He thought furiously at the little dragon about being ready to be out in the world. It stilled as if listening to him. He felt a slight and unwelcome pang of empathy.

It's all right, little monster. Time to go out into the world, that's all.

Some kind of viscous liquid dripped down his side. Then the movement started again, squirming and writhing underneath his skin directly against his muscles. He shuddered with disgust, his face too swollen to allow for a grimace. Then there was pain. Something attacked his flesh, straight through to his spine. The dragon tugged sharply, pulling at a connection between them that did not break.

"Help me, damn it," he croaked out. "Old woman, where are you? Help me."

The tug came again, more insistently, straining against sinews that were buried deep in Xeras's body. He couldn't move his broken left arm around and flailed to reach across with his right arm which was mottled with deep bruises, the fingers clubbed over with nails bloodied and torn.

His mind groped past a blurred memory of Drin and skipped guiltily to a sharp image of Duke Carly's face. He stilled. He could see Carly's warm brown eyes always so open and accepting. Despite his own barbed comments, his people were lucky to be ruled by a man who was, if anything, too gentle and compassionate, rather than the usual petty tyrants who rose to, or were created by, that kind of position. Power, as his father all too frequently said, is poison to character. Carly's expression did not seem to match that pronouncement.

Carly's moods were mild, his manner charming and what he saw in Xeras was beyond comprehension. Maybe it was simply an extreme case of opposites attracting. Xeras wanted to get back to Ballot's Keep. He wanted, if possible, to live there for the rest of his life. But this was hardly a useful time to dwell on that.

The pains redoubled, shooting not only through his torso, but arching out through his limbs like tendrils of fire. He tried not to move, but couldn't help but flinch and feel the protests of his injuries in response.

"Damn it, help me," he whispered too hoarsely and quietly for anyone to hear.

Tears formed in his eyes. Time seemed to stretch and crawl by. Sometimes he felt movement and excruciating pains that radiated through him. He would collapse, limp and dull with no thoughts. Waves of agony and exhaustion passed over him, drawing out the last of his strength until he could endure no more.

He began to accept that he *was* going to die here, alone in the open, in some wilderness whose name he did not know. The birds started to swell their calling, ruffling amongst the foliage, when he felt a rending sensation in his stomach and thick liquid burst out, spilling in a cascade down his side.

So this is how it ends. All things considered, his father had the right of it. Xeras had achieved nothing in his life and died poorly and in pain, failing those who depended on him. He could hardly have done worse by staying in Tirrin. But he recoiled from that conclusion. Even if it did nothing but doom him, he had to leave Tirrin for what had been done there. It was not a thing any man, any man whose feelings were true, could have endured or, by his continued presence, condoned.

A slight creak and scrape suggested that the door to the structure behind him had opened. Xeras did not react. He had no further expectations and no demands. Even as she knelt beside him, he did not look down. He could see above him the edge of her small cottage's roof and the sky very slowly leavening with dawn.

Something cold touched his side, inside some kind of ragged wound whose extent he did not want to know. She made one neat, precise movement and the thread that had so tortured him seemed to relax, contract and settle into a dull ache.

A sound broke through his awareness, something quite indescribable. Almost a peep, but more like a gasp. Something about it pierced Xeras and he could not help but care where it had come from. The old woman reached up and pulled down the lace collar of his tunic to expose his skin. She placed the creature there, small and wet. It moved feebly, four distinct scratching limbs pushing up until it was nestled under his chin. He could not see it but could feel it, about the size of a field mouse. A rapid pattering heart beat against his skin.

"Looks like you might live," was all she said, whether it be to the get or to him.

From her dwelling, the woman brought a bowl of thin stew which she maneuvered into his mouth, seemingly not greatly interested in whether he swallowed or suffocated. Then she went back inside and closed the door behind her.

The day slowly warmed and Xeras followed the light *tip tip tip* of the tiny heartbeat. He felt strangely peaceful. He had to concur. Perhaps he was going to live. Perhaps they both were.

Ↄ

Xeras's mind wandered between the living and the dead, specifically Drin and Carly. He had only just come to accept that he welcomed Drin's presence on his life, whatever form it took. And if Drin was now, just as inexplicably, gone again, he had wasted their extra time in disagreeable bickering. He hoped that was not so. He pledged to be more grateful for Drin's presence if it returned, but he felt a little cynical about such promises. It was hard to believe he had the kind of spiritual depth necessary to change his nature that radically.

And as for Carly, he could not say he knew the man. He was well made, kind and interested in Xeras, at least at a physical level. What did he feel about the man? A sort of distracted elemental attraction not informed by any particular understanding or familiarity. He had been given an opportunity there and, in a depressingly familiar pattern, he had squandered it.

For all that Xeras was feeling emotionally rather defeated, his battered body rallied. Even in the short time since the dragon had been so dispassionately detached from him, the swelling in his face had subsided. He could see from both eyes and although each breath still hurt, it was a dull ache not the stabbing pains of the previous night. In fact he had to assume that in his panic, he had rather overestimated the injuries he had suffered. Not that he was walking out of this benighted place anytime soon, but standing up didn't seem an impossible proposition. Or at least crawling into the shelter of the cottage before another chilly night descended.

In the warm midmorning sun, the mouse-dragon climbed feebly down from under his chin. It went as far as it could upon his skin then groped weakly at the edge of his tunic, reluctant to go farther.

He saw it clearly for the first time. It was pallid and pink, in shape like a drastically foreshortened gecko with flaccid wrinkled skin that lay in folds back from its shoulders. These, he presumed, were its nascent wings. It made its quiet piping call again. In answer the woman emerged from her home.

Xeras could see her now. Without doubt a very elderly

woman, she stooped with frail limbs and cobweb-fine white hair that fell down her back almost as far as the ground. She fixed him with a disdainful glare, ice blue eyes suggesting that his survival came to her more as an affront than a relief.

"It needs feeding. You should not have it healing you. It is too weak."

"Healing me?" He looked down at the small, fumbling creature on his chest.

"It needs feeding."

"Feeding with what? What do dragons eat?"

"Whatever it is their nature to eat," she replied curtly. "At this age it should still be within you for months, even many years."

"Then perhaps you should have told me to will it to have a stomach," Xeras snapped. The little dragon yawned, flexing its tiny toes. If it could indeed heal him even now, maybe he could still influence it. "You have made it quite clear that you are interested only in the dragon's welfare and not my own. And I for one will be happy to leave it with you. In the meantime, I am less than ambulatory, so I suggest you gather up anything you think a dragon this size might eat and we will do what we may."

The old woman merely grunted and turned away, walking around the back of the house. Xeras recalled dimly that the stone dragon had referred to her by name, but the name itself he did not remember, nor was he inclined to ask.

The little dragon seemed to peer nearsightedly in his direction, although its eyes were still tightly closed. "And cut it out with the healing," he said to it. "If you do yourself in with the effort, I don't think it would go well for me."

The dragon's head sank down again and it made some futile efforts to curl its short body up to rest.

C3

The woman had grudgingly produced a rustling straw-filled cushion to support Xeras's head and she provided food, bland but welcome. Leaving him this time with a spoon to manage as best he could with his less damaged arm and the bowl balanced on his chest.

The little dragon seemed more listless. It had been offered everything they could jointly think of and had at hand. Meat, bird's eggs, foliage of all types and several types of inorganic matter that the woman said some dragons ate—dirt, stone, wood. It gummed at and rejected each offering and refused to show any interest. It lapped feebly at both water and milk, but spilled it out again.

The dragon grew perceptibly weaker. Its body felt dry and cold, its palpable heartbeat slowing. Xeras wracked his mind. What did he need to do? With fledglings taken from the nest, one sometimes had to feed by poking food deep into the mouth like a mother bird would, but he would need to know he had chosen something that would be nutritious before resorting to force.

He thought fiercely to the dragon about throat, stomach and vent, and indeed it had all the outward parts necessary. The dragon lay quite still, barely alive at all. It was failing quickly, but small creatures often did. The old woman sat beside him on the porch, silent as ever but less impassive as she watched the dragon with him, seeing it fail and weaken. Xeras had one last thought.

"Bring me your knife," he said.

She looked at him accusingly and made no move.

Xeras stifled his irritation. He was at this woman's mercy and would have to try not to vex her more than necessary.

"If it is meant to be inside me, then its natural appetite should be for my blood. That must be what sustained it then."

"And a thin diet that must have been." But she reached around and pulled a small knife in a leather sheath from a pocket in her skirt. "Give me your hand."

"I'll do it myself."

She gave a pointed look at his left arm bound immobile to a wooden plank. "I doubt you have the gumption."

Drin might not be there, but Xeras could still hear his counsel. "I know you argue just for the sport of it, darkling. But just once, see sense." Xeras reached over, laying his hand palm up. There were plenty of scratches on it already, some quite deep, but others looked to have been healing for many days, not just a matter of hours.

She grabbed his hand and flicking the sheath off the small blade, stabbed it without restraint into the tip of Xeras's forefinger. He pulled back, exclaiming in wordless protest. The little dragon was dislodged and grabbing for it he stopped it from falling to the ground. Drops of blood splashed the woman's skirt and dripped onto the dragon and his own forearm and palm.

Even as he watched, the dragon's nares flared wide. It groped with tiny, trembling paws and its mouth settling on a drop of blood on his wrist. Its forceful sucking pulled at his skin.

His lacerated finger continued to bleed and he couldn't reach to redirect the little monster to a better source. Nor did it need the help. Xeras felt an insistent rasping pull and his flesh grow a little paler around the spot the dragon sucked upon; it had broken through the skin.

"Clever little get," the woman said. "Knows what it wants now, and how to find it."

"Yes, how lovely," Xeras replied faintly.

As he watched, the almost translucent skin of the dragon flushed from a pale shell pink to near magenta. He was beginning to feel rather alarmed at its capacity when it released him, wobbling back on a distended stomach.

"Are you ready to come inside now?" the woman said perfunctorily as she got laboriously to her feet.

ॐ

And so their days fell into something of a pattern. Xeras lay upon a makeshift pallet in one corner of her one-room dwelling. His body healed quickly in surges that followed after the dragon get's feeding. Its mouth left small circular marks up and down his arm, but they closed quickly and did not bleed. He ate whatever the woman gave him and drank prodigious amounts of water. The dragon grew more vigorous and, although it did not change in size or shape, it stood confidently upright and spread out wings, each one the length of its body from nose to tail tip, bones and flesh something like a naked bat. Finally its eyes opened to reveal small, featureless red orbs.

His host had an unmistakable fascination with the dragon that bordered upon reverence. As soon as it started to venture away from Xeras, she would try to coax it to her. He saw her surreptitiously provide it with her own blood, but it rejected this offering emphatically. The dragon explored around the room, but heeded the woman no more or less than any other object or piece of furniture. If she tried to hold onto it, it would start up with a piping cry that grew piercing and shrill as it gained in strength.

With a scowl, she would release it to scamper back to him where it would hide, nestled under his chin nervously until its curiosity won out again.

It was during one of these regroupings that the dragon, as yet still nameless, balanced upon Xeras's outflung foot, wobbling back and forth with wings spread for balance. The dragon fixed its gaze on an area a few feet away. It gave an entirely new kind of call. A kind of trill that rose up happily.

Their laconic host was outside on some errand she did not care to explain. Looking around Xeras saw nothing to elicit such a reaction.

But then you never were terribly perceptive, darkling.

"Drin, thank the Gods. I was worried."

The little dragon's gaze shifted, suggesting that whatever it saw moved slowly to a position beside Xeras. It scampered down his foot, along his leg and body in eager bounds with wing flared out. Then stopped, leaning out to stare fixedly at the empty air. Reaching up tentatively, Xeras felt the slightest brush, like a single strand of cobweb.

The energy welled up naturally within him and, as he watched, glittering strands and wisps rose from his fingertips, coalesced and formed into Drin's likeness. The dragon chirped its approval, apparently discovering a whole new vocabulary.

Drin stretched out his arms, flexing his fingers and examining his own hands and body. *A little clothing, I think? For the sake of the lady.*

As, indeed, this time Drin appeared, not clothed in his usual servant's tunic, but quite naked.

"I didn't mean to...I mean..."

Now you have that magic that you told Harus you never wanted.

"Oh please don't bring him into it." His father had been the subject of many an argument between them. Drin always chiding him for acts of purposeless rebellion against the only family he had. His father, the worthy conclavist, scholar and mage. The man he never quite forgave for being so distant during his solitary childhood years...

Even though he did try his best to close that gap once you were older. He never had any understanding of children. Some men are like that.

"Some women, too," the old woman said as she came back inside with a basketful of firewood.

So that creature he'd considered a delusion was now seen by everyone in the room. Although of course the dragon was bonded to him by blood and magic and the woman read minds—hardly a ringing endorsement. She snorted and went about her business as if the appearance of a ghost was an event of no particular note.

Some clothing? Drin prompted.

"Nothing I haven't seen before," the woman muttered as she shuffled by.

Xeras was getting the knack of...well, whatever this was. He pictured clothing in his mind. And it wasn't like in the past when a memory would be just a vague shadow of shape and color. He saw the robes his father wore for the conclave, with the fur trim and extra yards of cloth that hung in folds from his belt. He saw every detail and stitch. It never suited him really, portly man that he was, but adapted to Drin's height and breadth of shoulder...

And with a touch it wended up from his fingertip and encircled Drin. The wraith looked down, his expression somewhat blank. Then he scowled.

Don't jest with me. He tried to grasp the edge of cloth.

"I am not," Xeras said. "I always knew it would suit you. If people only served their due, rather than their station, it would have been me in the stable, or the attic, and you destined for greatness."

I never had the blood.

"What good did it do me? I never had the talent. Just the temperament. You know what they say about the high blood of Tirrin. It's a wonder the line breeds at all."

Get this off me.

And it was plain that Drin, for all his private confidence, was deeply uncomfortable, even afraid to be dressed as one of his "betters". But what was Xeras to do? Put him back in the rough tunic of a houseman. He couldn't make himself do that and not because he wasn't considerate of Drin, he thought more of him than that.

With an exasperated gesture and a puff of light, Drin vanished from sight. In a moment of pure terror, Xeras struggled to his feet. His side puckered and broke open bleeding and he wavered before realizing he still felt Drin's presence. He had simply dispensed with any visible image. Xeras turned aside, tears in his eyes, a relief strong enough to hit him as a wave of nausea.

He took a step back and felt the mouse-dragon slip from under his foot as he staggered to avoid treading on the damn thing. Xeras sat down heavily, but in one piece. The dragon, quite unharmed, climbed up his leg with its tiny hooked claws.

Xeras tried to tell himself he didn't care about any of it. Not the little monster. Not the old woman who clearly disdained him. Not the ghost.

I'm still here.

"Are you? When I have more control of your appearance than you do. How can I know I haven't been creating you all

137

along? Just getting better at it with the little boost the little monster here has been giving me."

Back to this again, are we? I cannot to be seen at all.

"That's not control. It's surrender. That's what you did all those years of playing the faithful servant. Tried to escape notice whenever you could."

While you fought your father on every little thing. Whether it mattered or not. Whether it was wrong or not.

"But I never really won. And I could do nothing for you."

I never expected you too. But I know that you tried.

Xeras sat in silence. The old woman moved around over by the hearth as if she didn't notice a thing. Maybe she didn't care, and why should she? We only care *about* the people we care for, in the end. Xeras was hardly in a position to criticize anyone else for not spreading her love around lavishly.

Drin would have been better off without him. Carly would be too.

Don't get into one of those moods. I can't talk to you when you get like this, like you are nothing and can do no good.

"What good have I ever done?"

We were good, Xeras. And you have it in you to be a good man.

And there it was. The only person who had ever loved him wasn't prepared to say he *was* a good man. Xeras lay back slowly into the dip his body had made in the rough pallet. The dragon scrambled laboriously up his body and nestled into its favorite spot just under his chin.

He remembered what the stone dragon had said to him about the type of person who ended up with a dragon get. A person in want of a reason to live. Perhaps this was one small thing that he could do. See this creature grown up and somewhere safe, make sure the accord was observed so that dragons did not so oppress the humans around them and the humans in turn did not hunt the dragons into extinction. Maybe that would be a good thing to do.

He wasn't entirely sure, and that bothered him more than anything. How was he meant to judge right from wrong when he had never really striven to do right before? The only good thing he had known was his time with Drin, and Drin had died because of it.

I'd do it again Xeras. Even knowing, I would do it all again.

"Oh, Drin, I was never worth it."

Oh, Xeras, that was never for you to say.

03

They settled into a kind of strained domesticity. Drin remained for the most part invisible, as if that was an argument he did not want to resurrect. Drin and the woman talked directly, more over the passing days. That was how Xeras learned her name was Marlha, last in a line of women who had much to do with dragons. Who, as tradition had it, had once served them as Xeras now did, only rather more competently. Wisewomen whose powers and prestige had faded with each generation, their heyday in a time before even the Tirrin expansion.

"...that magic comes to men as continuance to the serpent race..."

He was piecing it together. Magic. It came and went. The men of Tirrin clung to it, trying to breed together the last vestiges of their stolen treasure. And now he had some notion of where it was stolen from. There was no way to be certain, but his intuition was satisfied by the fragments and the picture they suggested. The only thing he did not understand was why Tirrin would surrender the power, let the bond lapse and thrust it into obscurity. Marlha obviously sought it still, perhaps honorably, but with avarice.

She had stopped bothering the dragon who clearly wanted to have nothing to do with her, but she watched it wherever it went. She whispered the words when she spoke to Drin about her lost heritage. She only wanted to serve the dragons, but Xeras suspected it was the magic she desired. He felt that magic stirring within him, dormant. He did not welcome it. Would it limit itself to troubling dreams and some nascent understanding of the stuff his ghostly companion was made of? Not that he had put either to good use. Magic took what form it chose and he did not want further turmoil in his life.

Xeras recovered his strength slowly. He started to make his way around the cottage. There was a meager garden out back and he made some feeble efforts at helping his host with it, but she impatiently pushed him aside, preferring to do things herself and perhaps pleased to rub in his own inadequacies. In truth Xeras knew nothing at all about raising plants or stock. He turned to Drin for advice and noticed with some interest that the wraith clearly knew many things that Xeras himself did not. Surely that meant it truly was Drin, who had been raised on a farm on the mainland before going into service on Tirrin. It vexed Xeras to fall so easily in and out of doubt. But losing Drin had been wrenching, had been so hard he flinched from thinking about it. Accepting his return meant, he knew, experiencing his loss again sometime. Even Drin had said so. He would only stay until he was happy that Xeras was whole, and he seemed uncommonly fixed on setting him up with someone—with Carly. He said he would never leave unless Xeras asked him to go. But he had said that once before. Such things are rarely entirely under one's control.

Xeras fed scraps to the few ragged hens that lived in a rough coop attached to the roof. They retreated there with a great flurry if he ever moved too quickly. The mouse-dragon followed them around with inexhaustible curiosity, receiving a few inquisitive pecks in return. Xeras straightened his back. There was a great ragged scar on his side and he grew tired quickly, but he had healed far faster than should have been possible. Perhaps he should not be so cautious of magic, but the one thing his father had taught him was that magic did harm more often than good. Raw power in men's hands was more likely to be made into a weapon than a boon.

Still, there were some advantages to having a dragon...what? Daughter? Familiar? Pet? Even as he stood it skittered over and clutched at his ankle, beginning the long climb up to its preferred vantage on his shoulder. He was getting used to having it around. After all, it had never asked to be here either and it was the agent of his rapid healing.

As well as the reason you were injured to begin with.

CB

Xeras stood on the front porch and looked out into the unilluminating vista of bare tree trunks and scrubby underbrush. He felt strong after a fashion. It was a fragile strength; he could not push it too far—like being made of glass. But he felt restless, too, and the urge to walk away from this place grew within him.

It continued to snow, steadily in fluffy drifts. The frigid air was hard to breathe, but the icy ache in his lungs was better than the stifling warmth inside. He knew, somehow, that it was time to go, though he knew he would not get far alone.

141

You want to get back to your impetuous duke.

"It is not what I was thinking of. But you are right. He's offering me somewhere to...be. Some place to make a home, have a life. And that is what I want to do. Would you mind?"

Mind, Xeras? You keep asking me that. Do I think I would want you to mourn me forever?

"I do mourn you, and I always will. And I have asked you about this a sum total of twice, counting this occasion."

My point is that you need not mourn me to the exclusion of all else. Of course I do not mind. If my approval makes any difference to you, you have it.

"Your approval is the only thing I ever really did want."

Apart from your father's.

"His? I think not."

Drin appeared faintly. He still wore the outrageous garb of an elder in conclave. With a thought Xeras changed it to the clothes Drin had worn in life. Their simplicity did suit him better, not distracting the gaze from his breadth of shoulder, strong-jawed face and wide brow over gentle eyes.

Looking at him, Xeras felt a lurch. If mourning no longer preoccupied him, it was because Drin did not seem entirely dead—just differently alive. He wavered. In this isolated place he could fix upon the idea of Carly as a prize or goal. A man he barely knew who offered a comfortable life, friendship... The real man was rather more complex and might have his own idea about things. Just because he made advances in the solitude of the mountainside didn't mean he was offering to set up house together.

The more he grew accustomed to Drin's unorthodox return, the more his feeling for him rekindled. If Drin was here to help him move on, he had a rather slow way of going about it. Xeras was, in this moment, more confused than ever. Perhaps Drin would do a lot more if he could. The ghost had explained that in trying to save Xeras from falling he had expended too much energy and been unable to reform for a while. Yet with time Drin grew stronger, became visible. What would he do if he really could touch and influence the world directly?

Xeras was on the verge of tracking Drin down to talk about the real nature of life after death when he saw a large shape moving through the early morning mists. A small part of the mountainside had detached itself to amble towards them. The stone dragon. The mouse-dragon huddling against his neck trilled its welcome.

Xeras curled his fingers over the rough balustrade. He could not reasonably resist whatever the dragon had come here to do—nor could he avoid trying.

"You wish to return home," Marlha said from the doorway. "Jarvice has come to take you."

"You knew he was coming?"

"The last vestige of my line's lost powers. I can tell when dragons are coming. I have some sense of what they mean to do."

Her bitterness was evident. "There are worse things, you know," Xeras replied. "I imagine you have led too good a life to serve as parent to a dragon. Ask your Jarvice about that. You have to be, as he said, in want of a reason to live. I imagine it makes this whole process a little precarious."

She looked away and went back inside. No doubt she would rather have suffered more and been rewarded with dragon magic.

No matter how grudgingly, she had been good to him. He could think of no way to thank her that she would accept. His father had always delivered such admonitions about the

143

dangers of power and maybe he had the right of it. It had warped the life of the woman without ever being within her grasp.

The stone dragon sat heavily in the small dusty area in front of the house. "The Bond of Hurn is in force," he said blandly. "The terms are met. I have come to return you to Tirrin."

"To where?"

"You are of Tirrin. It is your home. Your kind have bonded to ours before. It makes the process easier. You will find support and instruction with your people. You will experience changes now the bond is once again in force, as will others."

Xeras leaned forward. "Tirrin is *not* my home. I have repudiated all connection to that place. My home is Ballot's Keep and that is where I will go, with or without you."

Jarvice looked at him steadily. "That is a situation not without complications. But Ballot's Keep is as good a place to learn that as any, and significantly closer. Gather anything you need. By taking a path directly over the mountains we will be only two days in traveling."

Chapter Thirteen

You do not really sit *astride* on the back of any creature as large as a dragon. Even at the narrowest point near his shoulder, the flat top of his body was an expanse the height of two men. When he moved the dragon's whole body pitched steeply forward and backwards, and the terrain meant he also pitched and yawed above great chasms that made toppling from the yellow dragon's cache seem minor in comparison. Xeras was about as uncomfortable as he could imagine being.

For the most part, Xeras kept his eyes firmly closed. A row of spines projected from the dragon's skin, to which he clung grimly. Given more time to prepare, he would have suggested some method of attaching himself securely. He was pleased at Marlha's final thought, a padded drawstring bag in which a mildly aggrieved, tiny dragon was confined. It struggled against the confinement intermittently and it sulked about the whole thing with infantile persistence and incomprehension.

As they went higher, it got frigid enough to give him a whole new perspective on cold. It was becoming a rather depressing thread through his recent experiences. Holding on to his precarious perch became increasingly exhausting and he hoped the dragon's influence would keep life in his insensate extremities. The dizzying height terrified him beyond the point where his body and mind responded. And that in itself became a familiar sensation. Maybe that was all that bravery was, putting yourself in situations where you experienced terror and came out the other side, helplessness in the face of peril.

He opened his eyes briefly just as the dragon, Jarvice, lurched over the crest of a mountain range and tipped down the other side like a walking teeter-totter. Xeras made a desperate grab for the spine in front of him and barely avoided being pitched straight over. His terror proved resilient beyond any habituation and reasserted itself with a vengeance.

The bag tied around his neck pulled loose and flapped outward, swinging on the end of its string. The dragon get chirped its annoyance and began struggling again. Then the bag felt lighter. Xeras's eyes flew open just in time to see the get spring forward with its puny wings outspread. But he knew the damn thing couldn't fly yet.

Xeras lunged forward disregarding Drin's exclamation: *Neither can you!*

Which proved altogether too apt. Jarvice was now descending the steep ravine. The spine Xeras had clung to pressed against his chest by gravity, but in his desperate grab he slipped to one side of it. He reached back too late and, with recalcitrant dragon in hand, he slid along Jarvice's broad shoulder.

His free hand slapped on the stone dragon's hide, grabbed, scrabbled, slipped. He glanced down, looking for some place to land as he slithered over the craggy surface of the dragon's hide, but the closest thing he saw below seemed to be a cloud. His brain was calculating the one last decision he had, whether he should let go of the little dragon in the hope it would somehow manage on its own, whether its little paws and light body could find purchase where he couldn't...

He felt his body lift from the dragon's hide, and Jarvice's

great paw closed around his torso, plucking him out of the air with surprising alacrity. Xeras hung upside down looking at the steep and broken slope too precipitous even for snow to cling to.

"It is difficult," Jarvice said solemnly, "for me to make progress on three legs. Especially at this juncture. I am one with the stone, but the stone is not always one with the rest of the mountain."

Xeras wanted to say "how reassuring". But talking wasn't an option when facing such a view from such a vantage. Even breathing was quite difficult in such a tight grip, but he wasn't going to complain.

That's good, darkling. No need to argue with the dragon right now.

Jarvice continued on his way somewhat more awkwardly. Xeras closed his eyes and considered that there were always new frontiers of discomfort to discover.

ᚳ

Fortunately, he arrived in Ballot's Keep in a more dignified position midmorning of the following day. Jarvice had refused to expand upon his enigmatic comments about "complications". But Xeras received no response, just inexorable, plodding progress through two long days and two even longer nights.

Why would it matter if he was from Tirrin or claimed some other place? Surely taking responsibility for the get had implications for him alone and the obligation not to harry humans was a general prohibition? A good many possibilities ran through his mind, but without more input from someone better informed it meant nothing.

With some relief, he found his journey was finally at an

end. The snow was settling into the valley of the town, packed deeply against walls and houses. Muted smoke rose from the chimneystacks and frosty vapors blew through the great gate. That gate was something of an enduring puzzle. All in all Xeras was building up quite a stack of things he wanted to know a great deal more about.

Curiosity, as I have always said, is one of your defining features.

"Along with an oversized nose and unmanageable hair."

It suits you better, long like this, Drin observed. *I suggest you leave it that way. I further suggest that you get yourself in somewhere warm and stay there until I have time to forgive you for throwing yourself off a mountain, twice. I have to rethink ever having held the opinion that you are an intelligent man. I wonder if our physical relationship blinded me to your more obstinate qualities...*

Jarvice stumped down the gentler slopes to the outskirts of the village and progressed with considerable caution down the main street. The reaction of the populace was surprisingly muted. A few shutters creaked open and slammed closed. Sensible, really. What are you going to do if the dragon wanders down the main street, step out and offer it a cup of tea?

The road narrowed just short of Carly's place and Jarvice stopped. Unlike the more cautious residents, Chamberlain Parlen burst out the side of the building like he had a man-sized slingshot installed for just that purpose. He was clothed in a nightshirt that flapped behind him revealing a little more than Xeras really wanted to see.

Parlen peered up to where Xeras perched upon Jarvice's expansive shoulders. The dragon slumped slowly down, joints bending, chest sealing onto the cobbled street with an audible hiss, his head and neck curling and sinking flat until, with a final thump, he seemed more like an inconvenient outcropping of rock bursting up from the street than a living creature.

Patting the dangling bag under his tunic to reassure himself that his charge was still there, Xeras looked around for the best method to dismount. The little dragon was very disgruntled at her treatment. Her? Well yes, perhaps. Time would tell. Then he clambered down laboriously to put his feet gratefully on flat and stable ground.

Parlen's mouth was open like he intended to say something, but his brain couldn't settle on what it was going to be.

"The conversation with the dragon took a little longer than I had planned." Xeras straightened his clothes and stretching his cramped limbs. "Nor was it at a location of my choosing."

A body of people gathered, emerging from their dwellings. Pushing through them, the duke himself appeared. Carly rushed out, his eyes latched on Xeras greedily and he stepped forward with arms outstretched. Mindful of his now detached but still fragile passenger, Xeras retreated nervously, stumbling over the ridge of Jarvice's petrified paw.

"Well," Xeras forestalled. "The good news is that I did sort out an agreement with the dragons."

"Well that's dandy," Katinka said, appearing from behind her brother. She seemed a little startled to see him but not beyond the point of being glib. "Now perhaps you can do something about the Tirrinians."

"Certainly," Xeras agreed, matching her tone. "But perhaps after breakfast."

ℜ

It was rather late for breakfast but they were able to oblige. Xeras sat down to a reasonable repast with a significant audience. They gathered, not in the parlor, but in a private drawing room that he took to be Carly's by the way he sat confidently across the small table. Katinka invited herself in and Parlen refused to be excluded. Durrin also separated himself from the crowd and took on the task of excluding the rest of the onlookers.

The suite was towards the front of the house and before sitting, Xeras had peered out the window where Jarvice was content to be more of a fixture than a visitor. A number of children were already climbing gleefully up his sides, much to the displeasure of their parents.

It was good to have a soft chair under him and hot food appeared with great alacrity. Xeras ate with a steadily returning hunger.

And about time. We have enough to worry about without you starving yourself. That is the last adversity I would wish you to face, hunger.

But hunger was the feeling that had deserted him. For the longest time after Drin had died, Xeras ate only if he forced himself to. His stomach growled. Something else was moving, too. The dragon get turned. He would need to let the poor thing out soon, but this wasn't quite the right moment. The time had come. He needed to tell these people the whole truth and let them make their own decisions.

"My apologies, Carly," Xeras said between bites. "I did not expect the sudden change of venue, and I am afraid Lefty was a casualty of the process. But then it should surprise no one that diplomacy is not my strongest suit. Still, the dragons have agreed not to bother people or livestock any further."

"What about that one blocking the thoroughfare?" bristled

Parlen.

"I imagine he is merely ensuring you understand the human half of the bargain."

"And what have you promised on our behalf!" Parlen exclaimed.

That promise, of course, related to a certain entity who had worked loose the drawstring again and chose that moment to emerge from Xeras's collar and make an ambitious leap across the table which was somewhat miscalculated. The get ended up landing emphatically in a bowl of fruit preserve.

"Nothing too arduous," Xeras said mildly. He gave the bulk of his attention to his breakfast. "A little baby-sitting with this creature. Who can only get up to trouble on her own scale, which must be considered better than Plegura's mischief."

"Seras are you saying—" Katinka began.

"Xeras," he corrected.

"With a 'z'?"

"With an 'x'."

"As the Tirrinians spell it." Carly's expression would be normal for most men, but on Carly it looked cold.

Xeras watched him cautiously from the corner of his eye. "Yes, I am told there are *complications*. Perhaps you might explain."

"Well you were carried off by a dragon and presumed dead. So clearly *we* have a lot to explain." Okay. So Carly was, for the first time Xeras had seen it, genuinely annoyed. Xeras felt a stab of concern. He had wanted for so many days to get back here, to this man. But now his return seemed fraught and awkward.

"I told you, it took longer to arrange than I expected. And...and this..." Xeras caught himself almost stuttering over

Emily Veinglory

excuses before drawing up short. He had all but died several times and his reason for the whole thing had been that damn prophecy about Carly and Ghardis. It wasn't as if he had wandered off with a blithe indifference to everyone else's welfare. He hadn't intended to go at all.

Oh it was blithe indifference, perhaps, but it was to everyone's welfare including your own. More a matter of cluelessness than selfishness...

Well, thank you, Drin.

The young dragon sneezed as it extracted itself, made it to the edge of the table and promptly fell off the edge. Katinka gasped and grabbed for it, but missed. Xeras was not bothered. Falling off a mountain might be hard on the little monster, but the height of a table wasn't enough to damage anything that lightweight. He heard it scuttling across the boards and felt it climbing to sit on top of one of his feet. Katinka peered under the table with some fascination. She didn't appear averse to having the get added to her menagerie.

"It is really a baby dragon?" she asked.

"I am told I need to give it a name," Xeras said. "Nothing that has occurred to me so far is appropriate for repeating in polite company."

Carly stared at him with a sort of bemused, wounded look. But there were other things he wouldn't dream of saying with other people around. Things like how he really felt about Carly, or wanted to. Was it only wishful thinking that the duke seemed offended that Xeras was so standoffish?

When he saw you were alive, he probably did expect something more along the lines of a joyous reunion. What do you think you are doing to the poor man?

"So tell me how Tirrin has become involved in all this." Xeras *was* concerned about Carly's feelings. But he needed to

152

know what was going on, he needed to be able to assure Jarvice that the Bond of Hurn was truly in force and these people were going to honor it. Because, frankly, he was going to need their help.

"A representative arrived a short while after Carly's return," Katinka explained. "A Tirrinian courtier by the name of Kassius and six guards, armed and mounted. Not quite sure of your standing with your countrymen, we made no mention of you to them."

"That's probably just as well." Xeras chewed on his thumb nervously. Kassius was a son of a minor but noble house who had made a name for himself through rhetoric and sorcery and was set to be one of the youngest men ever accepted as a full member of the voting conclave that ruled the island. The guardsmen would be trained and disciplined soldiers and a serious threat to a backwoods town like Ballot's Keep. The question was, what exactly had brought them here? Kassius's main talent was in scrying, in finding people or objects with certain properties. But the conclave would need to be looking for something quite extraordinary in order to send a nobleman on such a long and dangerous journey, even with a substantial escort.

And beside that, Xeras had no interest whatsoever in speaking to one of his erstwhile countrymen. He had left that behind, the laws, the rules, the duties, the mannerisms... It was an entire culture built on a brutal indifference to the needs of the individual, by they high or low.

Xeras was reminded of Drin's reaction to being dressed as a nobleman. If Drin had been born a noble, he would have done as well as Kassius. He was well built, affable and charismatic. He would have been a diplomat or a politician. Perhaps Xeras, knowing nothing else, would have been content as a woodman's son in the quiet green expanses of the fief lands. Perhaps if the fates had put them in a place they were better suited to this all would not have happened. For what is tragedy but a thing done for all the right reasons, but in the wrong time or place. But the only words that actually escaped his lips were rather less profound.

"Oh hell," Xeras exclaimed. "He's not looking for me, is he?"

"Does he have cause to be?" Parlen asked in a tone just short of accusation.

"He will say only that he seeks a man who came into magic," Katinka said. "Perhaps found an object, encountered a wiseman or some other key to old knowledge. It is an altogether vague description. He is driven in his search and confounded to be stopped here in that the weather has begun to turn."

Carly added, "It seems the Tirrinians believe they have the mandate to regulate anything to do with magic. This Kassius and his men have been through the gate. Several times he has spoken to the people of the plains. People we have not always been on good terms with and who are choosing to camp much closer to our lands than has been usual in recent years."

"It is past time the gate was closed for the winter," Parlen said. The edge in his voice suggested it was something he had advised for some time.

Carly stood suddenly. He went to the door where Durrin waited on guard. "Durrin, if you will excuse us. I am sure what you have heard so far will be more than enough to satisfy your mistress."

"I never…" Durrin began to protest.

"All the same." Carly held the door for him and addressed Parlen. "Chamberlain, you also have duties to attend to and I would be obliged if you could do your best to ensure the Tirrinians are discouraged from coming to these rooms. Perhaps you might draw their attention to our visiting dragon. That would keep them occupied for a while. You may leave this"—he made a vague gesture that suggested Xeras was the *this* in question—"in my hands."

Once he had reduced the room occupants to his sister and Xeras, he turned. His face bore a stern expression that changed its aspect from resembling nothing more than an amiable farmer to something more suggestive of a warrior set to charge. He approached Xeras, one finger pointing firmly to his midsection. Xeras steeled himself, not knowing what was behind such posturing.

He has reason to suspect you as a spy, at best.

Drin swung rapidly from being a metaphorical shoulder to lean on to being Carly's best advocate. The ghost's goal was clearly to say whatever might drive the two of them together.

"The gate," Carly began.

"Should you..." Katinka attempted to interrupt.

Their voices blended together in Xeras's head as he struggled to understand.

"What choice do we have?" Carly said. It seemed he was building up not to interrogation, but candor. "Kassius is clearly up to no good. Winter is here, the plainsmen are massing and the gate..." He turned back to Xeras. "The gate that has protected this town and regulated this trade road for many hundreds of years will not close. I have pulled the hidden lever that dukes of this town have used across the ages and this time, this only recorded time, it has not caused the gate to close. Once this is widely known, the plainsmen will take the town. I believe that is exactly what Kassius has encouraged them to do. And what he would do in that eventuality I do not know. There are a great many things I do not know...and I expect that you could illuminate me on many of them. And so you should if you wish me to believe you are any ally of the people of this town."

"And if he is not, he now knows we are defenseless," Katinka added, although without any evidence of alarm.

"And if he is not, it was probably his doing in the first place and it is a moot point anyway. Would you like to actually say something about this, S...Xeras?"

Xeras leaned down and picked up the dragon get and wiped it off perfunctorily with the edge of the tablecloth. Yes, he was attached to the foolish creature. Maybe there was some hope that Carly would be as irrational, even in possession of all the facts.

"Xeras..." Carly pressed with patience that seemed to be wearing steadily through its final thread.

Xeras looked up, mind blank, mouth open and said the only thing he knew to say: "I am pretty much making this up as I go along. All I know is that making peace with the dragons, taking on this little monster has caused more magic to circulate. As the dragon believed my allegiance to be to Tirrin, it is altogether likely it has resurfaced largely there, perhaps to their confusion or alarm. It might be for that reason they sent Kassius here to work out what is going on. Once here, like any good Tirrinian, he would start to insinuate himself into everyone's business."

Carly rested both hands on the table and leaned forward. "Kassius says he was sent to deal with trouble that began at a very specific time. Which, if he is to be believed, would be equivalent to a day or two before we even met. So he was coming here *before* you were asked to intervene with the dragons on our behalf, and resurrect this agreement you speak of. It does beg the question of just why you came here, and whose goals you serve."

"Well, I had already sort of begun on that...project when we met. Inadvertently, as it happens. I just sort of fell into it."

His eyes rested on the churned-up fruit jelly in the centre of the table.

"Your eyes aren't green anymore." Katinka sat back on a wooden chair some distance away. Clearly trying to view things objectively.

Xeras's mood began to plummet. What exactly had he expected? To be welcomed back into the bosom of a warm family—with whom he had been acquainted a full ration of two days. And what had he done, burst in, chased off a dragon, had an awkward fumble on a mountaintop, apparently died and then his countryman had turned up to foment war on the borders, talking about wild magic while their enormous gate ceased to function.

Hell, he'd suspect himself of being up to no good based on that. He felt closer to despair over the whole ordeal than he had since the encounter with feckless Plegura out in the woods.

And this, darkling, is the moment to do something. These people, for reasons that are hard to divine, do care for you and do want to believe in you. Give them cause.

Which all led to one of those moments when everyone, living and dead, regarded him as if they were wondering why he hadn't said anything yet.

"And you have scars," Carly said. "On your face."

"Really?" Xeras responded mildly. "Dragons can be very presumptuous that way. Changing things around on my own body, moving me around the place at their whim. Just like enormous Tirrinians—deciding they have a...mandate, I think you said, to do whatever they see fit, especially when it comes to magic."

He sighed and settled back, trying to gather himself. Carly and Katinka watched, wearing matching expressions of

157

bemused concern. The dragon get jumped from Xeras's lap back onto the table and made a beeline for the preserves. Xeras only hoped she would develop a taste for it. Feeding the damn thing blood was a nauseating prospect not least because as he did it, it didn't feel wrong at all. In fact it felt great, blissful. It was something he could die doing without becoming alarmed in the slightest. He tore his mind free again.

"The Tirrinians want magic. If they are getting more magic their main concern is to seize control of the source. The source, as it happens, is me and the little monster here, and beyond that, the dragons. I haven't the faintest idea what is up with your gate. Magic and me are newly acquainted. I might be able to figure it out, but the odds are Kassius already has. He is a true seer, a scryer. He no doubt understood exactly what the gate was as soon as he saw it, and it is not impossible that the problems with it hark from Tirrin hedging their bets. I know how they think and they will likely try and get what they want from you. But failing that, negotiate with others who might, with their help, seize power here and be more amenable to Tirrinian demands."

Carly looked from Xeras to Katinka, who shrugged in a sort of "it could be true" way.

Xeras felt there was a delicate tipping point suspended between brother and sister. The silence dragged on and Xeras glanced up but dared not look for too long. If Carly was at all rational, he would probably hand Xeras over to Kassius and his men and be done with it.

"So what do we do," Carly asked.

Xeras's heart leapt. He was amazed it didn't jump right out across the table after the dragon which was squishing around happily again, but without any sign that it recognized its play area as a food item. That "we" seemed to include him. He seemed to be part of that "we". It took a little while to sink in and he wasn't sure he trusted his assumption. There was one way to know, offer a suggestion.

"If Kassius realizes I don't know what I am doing, we are in trouble," Xeras said. "So we need to throw him off, and then after dark take a subtle look at this gate of yours. Perhaps with Jarvice's help we can sort that out."

"Jarvice?" Katinka asked.

"The large creature impersonating a small mountain out in front of your residence. I realize what I am saying is hardly reassuring. It is entirely likely you would have been better off if I had never chosen to pass by this way. I have never intended to cause anyone trouble, although I doubt that is much consolation."

You cannot know that these troubles are really your doing.

But he rather felt they were.

Carly looped his thumbs over his belt and nodded. "None of us can do more than have good intentions and act as best we may."

"If the best thing I can do," Xeras offered hesitantly, "is head back down the road you found me on, you need only say it." It wasn't what he wanted, but that wasn't his call to make.

"Oh, no," Katinka said without hesitation. "We would never send you out into the snow."

"And besides," Carly added. "We need you. We might need magic however it comes, to deal with the plainsmen at arms. We also need someone who will have some notion what that devious Kassius hopes to achieve here with his stirring. We and the plainsmen have kept our uneasy peace many generations, but the records show us the cost of war between us. Back in the day before the migrations, our enmity was the reason the gate was built. It is imperative that the gate is returned to working order."

A peace that depends on a wall. I wonder if that is peace at all.

Cynicism from Drin, now that was a worrying thing.

"I best speak to Kassius," Xeras said. "But not as I am. Appearances are important with my kith and kin. I must speak to him as an equal and as a citizen of this town, not a countryman. If that is what I am."

He did not quite phrase it as a question, still clutching to that tenuous *we.*

"I will announce an audience," Carly said. "To speak with our visitor. But I need you to think on this. If you are a citizen of this town, meaning to speak on our behalf, I will have your pledge as my retainer. I will have your promise of veracity and loyalty. And I know that is not a thing you want to give and perhaps you take more seriously than many men would. But if I am to trust in you, perhaps you need to trust that I would not abuse such an oath. That I would never hold you to it to your detriment. Do not answer me now. But think on it."

Xeras suspected Jarvice would require this also, a ritual tie from him to the people he claimed, if only to erase his connection to Tirrin.

So do it, Xeras. To truly leave Tirrin, you need to really arrive somewhere else.

☙

And so Xeras found himself back in that bathtub. Katinka herself combed out his hair, not like a servant would—perhaps as a sister. Still, the situation made him uncomfortable. She spoke to him with familiarity he presumed was normal in families. But then, she always had.

"So straight." She ran a wooden comb through the whole uncut length, tugging at stubborn knots. "And fine. Any woman would be happy to have it...other than the odd grey hair."

With that she grasped the errant strand between her fingertips and plucked it out with a flick of her wrist.

Xeras did his best to suffer her attentions without behaving ungraciously. "I should cut it to a length typical of men in these parts."

"I think not," Katinka said in a way that sounded more like a decision than a suggestion. "You may want Kassius to see you as a native here, but the villagers will be more impressed if you style yourself a little apart. Like the wisewomen in tales who used to walk the land and work magic. They always had long, wild hair."

She fluffed his hair experimentally with her fingers, but it simply hung, heavy and damp. He was struck with an image of what his father would think, styling himself after wandering women. In Tirrin only servants wore their hair long.

Carly joined them with a swathe of dark clothing folded over his arm.

"'Tis fortunate we said nothing of you to Kassius," Katinka continued. "I confess it was partly because we feared he might blame us for your untimely demise, but it allowed us to present your return as we wish."

Glancing down, the duke's brow furrowed. "You have picked up a few scars in other places too, I see," he said in a light voice strained with undertones of concern.

"I'm fine, Carly. Stupidity has its consequences and, all things considered, I could have done worse."

And might yet do very poorly in some areas if you don't let him know how you feel.

Carly stared at the ragged scar on Xeras's side. Objectively speaking, it was quite impressive, as wide as two fingers side by side, long, ragged and raised. The kind of wound most men wouldn't survive. If a man was ever going to show a depth of concern for another, that scar was just cause.

"How can it be healed over in this time?"

"A little dragon magic."

"And how did it happen in the first place?"

Xeras focused on scrubbing off ground-in dirt and, once again, as much skin as had to go with it. "The yellow dragon, Ghardis, decided to hide me away somewhere inaccessible. I was trying to escape when I had something of a fall. Then Jarvice, the grey dragon, brought me back here. He and I still need to have a conversation about just what has to happen for the Bond of Hurn to be considered in force and just what the implication of that will be."

Carly finally tore his eyes away. "These clothes are mine. Bring the belt in a few notches and it should serve."

He gave a look to Katinka that even Xeras could interpret as a request for privacy. Katinka blithely ignored him.

"I hate to say this, brother dear. But you two should wait until we have settled the most pressing of our affairs of state. Whichever way your private matters may go, it will not help with what we have to deal with here."

"Katinka," Carly exclaimed, surprised. "How can you be so...!"

The dragonling had clambered doggedly to the side of the tub and, startled by a raised voice and with a surprised squeak, it toppled in. Katinka made to grab for it, but given that it was sinking rapidly towards his groin area Xeras made sure to get there first.

He fished out the damp, pink creature with its sodden wings hanging down. Xeras held it in his cupped hands. *Her.* It did seem female and if not, then it was as good a thing to decide as any, his mind apparently having a role in her physical shape, if not her behavior.

"I am the last person who should be looking after her." Xeras hoped to distract them both from an untimely conflict. "I haven't even thought about a name. I've almost killed the damn thing a handful of times. And without her, there is no agreement, dragons are running wild again and whatever Kassius is up to with his arts, we won't have our own to counteract it."

"So, think of a name," Katinka said. "And get dressed. We don't have much time." Xeras looked at the dragon get. It appeared much the same as it had on first emerging, perhaps a hair larger and better coordinated. Small, pink, like a cross between a mouse and a newt, with bat wings added on top and a spurred end to its tiny tail. Objectively speaking, not an attractive creature. But it sneezed again, checking his position with tiny red eyes and Xeras knew he was not caring for her just for ulterior reasons, not anymore. The way the dragon get stayed near him, depended on his protection, kindled a response he could not deny.

"Drinia, then," he said.

Why, Xeras, I'm touched.

You always did want children.

∛

Xeras inspected himself in the mirror. Katinka had

arranged his hair in a tight braid that fell, shining and damp, down his back to his buttocks. He wore a long tunic in midnight blue cinched with a black belt. His black boots and leggings were passable, in that they were mostly concealed. The overall effect was severe, not least because of his gaunt face and stark white scar that now bisected his right brow and glanced off his cheek. His must have come closer than he supposed to losing that eye. Which was, at least, back to its usual muddy brown color. He looked...

He looked...

Battered? Starved? A little crazy? Trust me, darkling. You should take the offer you have here, rather than hope to find another well-provisioned young man with a taste for eccentric indigents.

I am not the only one to consider, Xeras thought pointedly at Drin. He was going to have to explain about the ghost sometime, too. But now was very much *not* the time.

"Drinia has not been away from me since she was...hatched," Xeras said. "But best if we keep her a secret for now. Though if I leave her, she might make something of fuss."

"I will stay with her," Katinka offered. "I will take her with me to the gate chamber and await you. I can make the preparation for closing the gate so that we might try it one more time. But you must ensure Kassius is nowhere near you before you join me there. Carly can show you the way."

Katinka seemed different from the carefree woman he had met a few weeks before. Her manner was not so different on the surface, but there was a tightness in her voice, a concern that ran through her like tension in a wire. She knew that dangers loomed all around and it was twisting her inside. Carly too.

Xeras turned to her. "I don't know that I will be able to help with that. The dragons have freed some magic, and some of it is coming to me. But I have no more than the most basic of educations in those arts, for I did not demonstrate that talent before. Unless the matter is quite simple, it may yet be beyond my means."

Katinka relaxed marginally. "We each do what we can. Nothing more can be asked."

And he wanted so badly to be able to do it. To solve their greatest problem, close their gate against a hostile neighbor, deal with Kassius and his men like some mythic hero. He thought it so horribly unlikely that he could rise to such heights. But she was right. What could he do, but try?

Carly held the door. "Will you swear your allegiance then?"

You already love him. This is a far simpler matter. Why do you hesitate? If this problem is to be solved, it will not be by you acting alone. Experience has demonstrated that.

And it was, after all he had been through, surprisingly easy to say, "If you'll have it. You may find it more of a handicap than an asset."

"I'll take it," Carly said. "Now Kassius will come to the audience hall, probably late, if at all. He shows scant respect to anyone here. But I need to know what he is up to, if it is he holding open the gate and if so how to stop him."

Coming up beside him in the open doorway, Xeras tried to put everything in his eyes. The pull he felt from Carly's solid presence, his desperate doubts that he deserved any consideration on a personal level or...that he could do anything at all about this mess. But he drew himself up tall, nodded, and walked on.

As it turned out, they needn't go as far as the hall. Parlen gestured to them and, looking out the unshuttered forward window, they could see the tall Tirrinian on the street. Every inch a true scion of Tirrin, Kassius was tall and fair. He

165

eschewed fashionable curls for a soldier's cut, short and close to his head, perhaps in concession to a hairline that was not so much receding as in full retreat. That same restraint was not evident in his clothing. He was dressed up in true Tirrinian style with an over-robe closely embroidered, complex belt hung with sword, and dagger impressed with enamel and jewels. His hands were covered by tight gloves, his feet by tall, shining boots. Quite how he got himself this high up in the hills in such pristine condition, Xeras could not imagine, but it probably had something to do with the ring of liveried guards that surrounded him.

Xeras made his way to the door. Kassius's attention fixed on Jarvice, who was—even to the discerning eye—looking particularly inert. Kassius's face was set in a petulant scowl, although he managed to look handsome with it. Of course Kassius looked handsome no matter what he did. It was one of his more irritating qualities.

Kassius's fists clenched and he glanced over at Xeras. "I should have known your father would have something to do with this." And then he turned his attention back to the dragon.

Xeras stood for a while. Surprised that he was surprised. He had never been seen as anything other than his father's disappointing inability to produce an heir that was a credit to him. You'd have thought the old man would remarry and try again, but he never did.

But Xeras had actually been away from the island long enough to become used to people, for better or worse, dealing with him as his own man.

Maybe time to get used to being one?

Kassius tried futilely to get some response from Jarvice. He stood quite dramatically with one arm outstretched, palm facing the dragon. Xeras could dimly feel the energy that emanated from Kassius's body and ran over and around the dragon's form. Finally Kassius pulled back.

"This dragon is dormant," Kassius declared. "It is unresponsive to anything we may do and will not move, probably until the spring."

"Jarvice, perhaps you could move out of the roadway," Xeras said mildly. "If you are staying with us a while you might consider the area out behind the duke's residence."

Almost immediately Jarvice raised his blocklike head and opened his eyes. Somehow his eternally motionless facial features conveyed bored tolerance. Several of Kassius's guard stifled amused smirks.

"I should concentrate on the task of reforming the bond," Jarvice remarked. "I was quite prepared to consider Tirrin partnered to our kind."

"I don't recall ever telling you I represented Tirrin."

Jarvice sighed and wrenched himself to his feet in a series of distinct stages, dust and small pebbles cascading off his body. The dragon limbering his short wings. Xeras wondered why he had wings at all when they couldn't have a function. Perhaps it was just that years ago some get-afflicted person thought all dragons were meant to have them. That seemed to be the way it worked.

Jarvice looked down, "So you will be formalizing your relationship to this realm? Magic abides best by ritual. So by the time the nascent magic has redirected its attentions from Tirrin to Ballot's Keep, it would be best if a sworn citizen of the realm abided by the bargain, or I will not answer for the consequences."

"I will get right onto that, Jarvice," Xeras said, unsure just who an enormous magical dragon would answer to anyway. "It's been a little busy lately."

"Yes, well. I've not been entirely unoccupied myself, walking over mountain ranges, returning human magic to the world."

It took a few moments to register that the dragon was matching his tone, arch as it was. He had gone through the process of discovering they still existed, being impregnated by one, raging at them, being abducted, being almost killed and apparently things were settling down into a little light repartee. Maybe he was about ready to start being a father of one.

And you call me a master of the obvious.

Jarvice eased by and made his way past the stable, looked the crumbling cliffside up and down and settled himself again. Within moments, his body hardened into jagged lines imperceptible from the surrounding rock.

"The audience chamber is this way," Xeras said with an airy wave of his hand. He held his head high and focused on being his father's son. Certainty. Privilege. If curiosity was, as Drin said, the key to Xeras's personality, his father's core was absolute assurance and belief in himself. He never doubted and he never explained. The will of Harus sometimes changed, but never wavered, and in the end, despite the many voices heard in the conclave of Tirrin, Harus's wishes tended to prevail, even though he was far from the most senior, feared or wealthy of their number.

Kassius did not follow immediately, but Xeras kept on going. Durrin opened the door into the small receiving chamber. At one end was a token dais supporting a single carved chair that Carly seated himself at. The open area of the hall was overlooked by high windows that threw stripes of light across the floor. Raised balconies were mounted down the side walls. To the far end of one of these, just over the door they had entered through, the Thurstian duchess and young Phinia were seated.

Xeras went deliberately to Carly's side, laying his hand upon the carved arm of the duke's chair. Durrin stayed at the door with nothing but the empty expanse of the room between them.

"He has just come from through the gate," Durrin said dourly.

Carly looked grim. Whoever these plainsmen were, they clearly represented a serious threat to the town.

And is it really your concern, darkling? Drin's voice sounded different, without a trace of its usual humor.

Could it be anything but his concern? Perhaps it flowed from a stumbling error in the darkness of the forest, but the consequences were his to own. The Bond of Hurn would be rehonored. Magic was coming, if not to Tirrin then to Ballot's Keep. And where magic went trouble tended to follow. How could he know what was the right thing to do?

Xeras had time to think on it as Kassius took his own sweet time. But he did finally step into the hall, stripping his gloves off in a precise, fastidious manner. Xeras felt, looking at Kassius's face, that this display of pique was just for show. Kassius was flustered. He did not have the manner of a man in control. Xeras focused on letting the tensions out of his body, standing at ease and pretending he didn't have a worry in the world.

Kassius would know from what he had just heard that Xeras had an agreement with the dragons, and that he was claiming Ballot's Keep as his home. The question was how much Kassius knew about dragons, and about the magic they bestowed and on what basis. It was possible he had journeyed here to find the cause of the resurgence Jarvice had sent their way, without knowing exactly the cause.

Don't give anything away, Xeras. Play for time, get him to talk.

Which was all very well, but apparently Kassius had the same thought. He stood before the duke's chair in perfect silence for a long moment. Finally Kassius spoke.

"It is you who called this little meeting. Perhaps you might bestow upon me some inkling of your reasons."

Phinia's eyes, Xeras noticed, were fastened quite firmly on Kassius. Fixedly, in fact. The duchess monitored the scene more generally with noncommittal interest.

"My duke," Xeras replied languidly, "finds your presence here vexatious. And what vexes him, vexes me. And what vexes me, vexes the honorable dragon Jarvice. Perhaps you might save us all some unnecessary perturbation by stating your business clearly, and returning to Tirrin."

Kassius laughed sharply, once, like a bark. He slapped his gloves across the palm of his hand as if giving the proposal polite consideration.

"Oh, I will return to Tirrin, and you will accompany me. You are the property of Tirrin, a citizen at the beck and call of the conclave. And everything that is yours, is ours."

Kassius's expression was unbearably smug. It was hard to know exactly where he got his confidence from other than by a long habit of privilege and his small force of men, an uncertain prospect against a village even of untrained men.

But Kassius had not seen Phinia and the duchess seated in the balcony above the entrance, or the expression on Phinia's face. It rather confirmed Xeras's first impression that the princess had formed a new attachment in his absence. If anyone could impede the Tirrinian's plans it was Phinia's mother.

"Ballot's Keep has its charms," Xeras said. "As I am quite sure you would agree. I do not find myself in any hurry to leave.
170

And it will be a simple matter to pledge my allegiance formally, severing any ground the conclave has for forcibly repatriating me. So do not presume to dictate my actions. I am done with dancing to the conclave's tunes."

Kassius did look somewhat uneasy. "You are, as I am, born of a high house of Tirrin. We will both remain, at the conclave's pleasure, members of that house with all attendant duties and responsibilities. We *will* return, you and I, to Tirrin, as our mutual duties dictate. Mine to carry out my orders, you to explain your outrageous conduct to those who will suffer the repercussions. And we need not delay."

Kassius made a gesture and two of his guards stepped forward, striding down the length of the hall with their hands on their swords. Phinia stood in the balcony, her voice little more than a gasp.

Call to Jarvice, Drin urged, but it was another voice that stopped them.

"Kassius, you promised I could go with you."

Kassius spun, startled and his men hesitated.

"Go with you?" the duchess echoed her daughter quietly. "Truly there must be something in the water in this town that makes men so presumptuous."

"Madam," Kassius forestalled. "I have not the luxury of time to explain, but my intentions are honorable. I must see to my duty first, before petitioning your husband for Phinia's hand."

Miscegenation, Xeras. Tell her...

Xeras needed no such prompting. "Were you so devious as to suggest that you would be allowed to marry her? The conclave would never allow you to marry outside the high houses of the Tirrin. If you did so without their blessing, your bride would be killed by their command."

Kassius turned to him. "Don't you see," he exclaimed with satisfaction. "It is because of you that they *will* allow it. You can tell the dragons to return new strength to the houses of Tirrin, new magics, new powers. There will be no more need to so zealously conserve our dwindling arts, so long as the dragons abide by you, and you abide with us. Once I have done my duty, the way to my happiness will be clear. I will be the savior of the magic of the high houses of Tirrin and Phinia will be mine."

And Phinia, by her clasped hands and joyous expressions, seemed entirely thrilled with that display of fervent cunning. The duchess's expression remained judicious as she placed a restraining hand upon her daughter's shoulder, like a falcon pinning its prey.

Carly stood now. He glanced to Durrin, who in turn watched the duchess for his orders. Ballot's Keep was not a town to keep any standing force of soldiers. Xeras imagined the citizenry saw to their own defenses as required, but if Kassius acted quickly they would not have time to respond.

"And if I stay," Xeras said with a smile, trying to exude ease and confidence. "What could you possibly do with a handful of men against a town that would benefit from retaining my influence for themselves."

The rest of Kassius's squad were inside the hall now, arrayed behind him in a grim line.

"There is no need to make this difficult, Xeras," Kassius replied.

And if Xeras was trying to act as if he was in control, Kassius believed he was. His face tilted up, smug and satisfied, and the reason was soon clear. "There are people living just through that defile to the north who have a long list of historical grievances against this town and the whole of the lowlands beyond. One of them in particular has rallied a great force with ambition to live a different kind of life. And *she* has agreed to align her interests with that of Tirrin in return for our patronage and assistance. So if you do not surrender yourself to me, you deliver this entire town to them."

Carly's whole body stiffened. The threat hit home. Kassius either knew or was responsible for the gate's malfunction. They were totally screwed.

What choice remained?

"And could you guarantee the town's safety if I did go with you?" Xeras said.

No!

"Xeras, no." Carly laid his hand over Xeras's where it still lay loosely over the arm of his chair.

Xeras watched Kassius so closely he could feel the subtle forces move between them through the empty void of the room. Kassius looked at him sharply as if he felt the energies connecting them.

"Yes," he said. "I am holding the gate open; I can allow it to close."

And he lied. As Kassius scried him, Xeras read Kassius in his own rough and untutored way. Xeras knew Kassius was lying, and Kassius knew he knew. They watched each other for a long, frozen moment. The only chance they had of returning the gate to its proper function was if Xeras stayed. He would have some access to the magic that worked the gate, as would others once the Bond of Hurn was fully in force. Without it, they would have no option but to hope the plainsmen did not invade. And he was willing to bet that having been raised to a warlike pitch, they would not so easily be dissuaded.

"They would have no reason to," Kassius said, advancing. "If you return to Tirrin. I will tell the plainsmen there is no need to invade the town."

The energy between them flowed and was buffeted back. He could not tell if Kassius was lying now, but that in itself seemed to be a deliberate evasion. Nor was it plausible that he could call up and call off a whole people like a pack of trained dogs.

"I think not. You have set things in motion. Endangered this town and anyone who remains in it." He looked up to Phinia, who leaned forward from the small balcony. Her eyes shone with a potent mix of trust, love and fear that lent a fascinating glow to her delicate features. He wondered if Kassius truly returned that regard.

"Phinia will return to Thurst with her mother." Kassius gestured impatiently for his men to continue their advance. He scowled to be pressed into an admission of the peril.

Carly stood, wielding the full if uncertain force of his authority but carrying no weapon more threatening than a dagger. "The door to your back to the right," he said in a low voice. "To the end, the stairwell and to the top. Bar the door. If you meant a word of your promise of allegiance do not baulk, do not even hesitate."

Go, quickly, go. For once, do as you are told.

Xeras stepped back. His eyes surely gave away his plans.

"Seize him," Kassius yelled.

Mindful of the difference between bravery and stupidity, Xeras bolted for the door. He slammed it shut catching a glimpse of Carly intercepting the closer guard who did not quite dare to draw his weapon.

The stone corridor beyond was low, dark and featureless. He stumbled down it, fingers running along the wall. At the end, a stair spiraled out of sight. Stubbing his toes against the narrow steps, he headed up and up. The stair was so much longer than he expected, wending through the darkness. Under his fingers it now felt as if it was not built up from separate stones, but chiseled from raw rock.

Gasping for breath he paused, almost on all fours on the steep narrow stairway.

Keep going until you can get that barred door between you and Kassius's men. Go.

"Easy for you to say," Xeras gasped. But he went forward, now in total darkness, groping with his fingers, feet slipping on the slick stone.

I hear them, on the stairs.

Xeras propelled himself onwards with new strength. The last thing he wanted was to be caught in the dark like a rat. He hit a solid barrier, rebounding off with a curse, cradling his arm. His left arm still felt uncertain, he wasn't sure how far it had healed and how much it would take to break it again.

With his right hand, he found the face of a wooden door, planked so tightly no light came through. It was cased with metal and seemed to be featureless, but putting his shoulder against it, the door shifted slightly. He barged forward and flung it open.

Xeras staggered into the light. Squinting he saw his feet just inches from the end of a hewn ledge. All around was natural rock. It folded in around him, but dropped off. He caught a glimpse of the stable roof far below before swaying back into the doorway. Looking around, he saw no way forward until he leaned and pulled the door inwards. Behind it a narrow open path led gradually upwards to the gate that loomed above.

"Damn it." The fates seemed inclined to toy with him and his fear of heights.

It is good to face your fears, darkling.

"I was under the impression that I had met my quota for

falling from high places. Especially as there is no dragon handy to catch me on this occasion."

Given the choice between a path that looks wide enough to be passable and a passage blocked by armed and hostile guardsmen, I would opt for the path. Besides, dragons are not currently in short supply.

"Given that the guardsmen aim to take me alive and the fall to the valley floor is less discriminating, I am not sure I agree. And as for..."

A flicker over the shrouded sun caused Xeras to look up. The sky was hung with low cloud but against it dark shapes shifted in silhouette. Two of them, the wide canvases of their wings passing overhead in lazy spirals. Together with Jarvice who, even if he could fly, would not have such an elongated silhouette, suggested three dragons gathered in the close confines of the township of Ballot's Keep. That could not be good.

It is what the duke asked of you, Drin pressed. *He would not put you in danger.*

"He has a very peculiar way of showing it," Xeras muttered. But he edged the door inwards and skirted around it onto the path.

The smooth stone was spotted with moss and debris; obviously not much in use. The door had pushed back a layer of dirt and scraped only reluctantly back in place. Xeras clawed down the hinged bar into its brackets. It struck him as strange to have the door set to be barred from the outside. Looking up towards the gate, he wondered what he would find there.

Let's go and find out then. But carefully. Don't mistake my endorsement of the duke's plan as a suggestion to run amok as you usually do.

"As I what?"

Irritation made it easier to try to disregard his thumping heart. Hugging the irregular surface of the wall, he edged forward. The path actually sloped outwards, as if encouraging him to fall. The path dipped and curved and stretched on, its precarious surface making the pitch-black stairwell preferable by comparison. Time wore on and he made poor progress. Perhaps it was like carrying water. If you went slowly, it was sure to be spilled along the way. Sometimes you just had to trust your balance.

Other people, maybe. Your sense of balance is atrocious. On that basis, your fear of heights is not irrational.

"Thanks for the vote of confidence."

Confidence is something you could use. Stupidity you have enough of. Stick close to that wall.

Somewhere up ahead, he heard the faintest suggestion of a sound, a peep. Drinia. Having a goal ahead of him, Xeras strove on. His fingers were slick with sweat, the ground always uncertain underfoot. But if Katinka waited for him, and Drinia, and maybe Carly, then he had to get there and soon. He had to swear allegiance to the duke. It was the only way. Once done, the Tirrinians would not benefit from the dragon magic. They could seize him, but it would do them no good. Even if they did, the arts would spring up in others at Ballot's Keep, giving them a way to defend themselves against any odds.

Wild magic would cause chaos, no doubt about that. Magic in the hands of people not used to wielding it. It would be a difficult time. If only he had never come this way. They would all have been so much better off. The guilt clutched at Xeras, distracting him so it took a moment to realize his shuffling foot felt a sharp edge beneath it.

Looking down, he saw how a great chunk of the hillside had fallen, the remnants of it caught in the cliffs and crevices below. The path was gone entirely for the height of two men, perhaps more. Perhaps he could jump it, with a good run up.

On a wet track with only a tiny space to land.

"You told me to come up here, dammit," Xeras whispered. "How do I go back? How do I go on?"

"How am I supposed to complete the bond if you persist in interrupting me?" Jarvice came over the crest of the hill. He tilted his great head, considering the crumbled cliffs of rotten rock. "The footing is not satisfactory. It would have been better if you called me before beginning the traverse."

"I don't believe I called you at all."

"Your fear calls me. Your peril is the get's. It cannot yet live without you."

Well, isn't it nice to be appreciated.

"Quite," Xeras commented. Nevertheless he looked at Jarvice and the crumpled, fragmented face of the cliff. "What would happen if you fell?"

"Some people below might be injured," Jarvice intoned. "The duke's residence would almost certainly not sustain the impact without a significant degree of collapse."

Jarvice could go down and warn them of the danger before making the attempt, clear the area below of people.

"And warn Kassius's men; tell them exactly where to look for me. Besides, I don't think falling off this cliff with a dragon would be much better for me than doing it alone."

"I have the solution." Jarvice turned laboriously, dangling down his great barbed tail and peering around to aim it. Spines the size of a man's arm protruded from its gnarled end. "I can convey you across, thusly."

Xeras took one last look at the drop below. If he fell, there was no way the dragon could catch him. But he heard that distant peeping again and had to go on. Wiping his hands on his tunic, its proud fabric now marred by dirt and sweat, he reached out. He grasped the jagged appendage as securely as he could, then wedged his foot over the final spur.

Carefully, Drin urged.

"I was not going to counsel same haphazard wagging about," Xeras replied, then addressed the dragon more loudly: "Let's go, slowly."

Jarvice swayed his heavy tail ponderously but with due care to the other side of the break in the path. Xeras clambered off. From here he could see the end of the path, sloping steeply upwards to an open archway in the side of the gate.

"It is almost time," Jarvice said.

"Time?"

Time to get your ass off this trail.

"The Bond of Hurn," Jarvice said patiently but not without a hint of exasperation. "You are the focus. Your people the beneficiaries of the arts of magic."

"But you aren't actually allowed to bother *any* people, right?"

"Quite correct. Unless of course the focus is lost, or has no people. Then all my efforts will be for naught and the dragons can do as they may. And there are those who would be most pleased with that."

Jarvice tilted his broad head upwards. The skin of the dragon throat seemed more pliable than his craggy ventral surfaces.

"Such as..." Xeras prompted. But Jarvice was not listening. Loose rock cascaded down in the wake of his passing.

Xeras pressed against the wall, feeling a scatter of shale and stones clatter off him, pieces bouncing from his shoulders.

He tried not to think about how this piece of the path might be just waiting to plunge from beneath him like the missing stretch. A final cascade of sand and detritus spilled over his head. Fate was determined that he be ragged and filthy.

Consider it a lesson in vanity.

"I was always unattractive," Xeras snapped. "Being tidy was pretty much the only virtue of appearance on offer."

You were always untidy, too. Hair springing up in all directions, ink on your fingers, and your posture...

"I just want to know which dragons we have in attendance," Xeras interjected.

Glancing up he saw one of them pass much lower, sliding over the gate like a shadow in the sky. It was Ghardis. Definitely a bad sign. Jarvice might be helping of his own will, but something told Xeras it would take the full force of the bond to win the yellow dragon's compliance.

"Not good." He continued to shuffle along.

Which doesn't really make much of a change, in terms of our recent mutual history.

"You mean since you died."

From a little before that, I should think.

Xeras stopped. His mind flashed back and it was as if his whole time since he had left Tirrin melted away and he was standing in the darkness again. In the darkness, in the cell with his father behind him and on the narrow pallet before him an almost unrecognizable body. Huddled, wizened, but still with that tumult of hair glinting in the dim light. He had leaned over to see the face, turned towards the wall. Even gaunt and pale he knew Drin's face. He touched a finger to his cheek, hard and tight against the bone.

Don't think about this now, darkling. Don't think about this anymore. It does no good.

And what good had Xeras ever done, no matter how he strove? He stared at his fingers clenched over the bulking cliff face and it didn't seem real. It didn't seem real or even likely that he had run away from home, been haunted by a ghost, gave birth to the dragon, grappled with a handsome duke on a barren mountainside, promised to try and magically repair a monument greater than any known race of men could have constructed.

Xeras.

There was a small fern growing from a tiny crack in the rock next to his hand. One of its tiny fronds dangled, freshly broken.

Xeras! Move. Get down this path, now.

He turned and looked up the path. Drin's likeness stood there, hand outstretched. But if he really wanted to be reunited with Drin he need only step the other way, out sideways into the void. Xeras was somewhat bemused at his sudden detachment. He had to help Carly and Katinka, and even the little dragon get. At least he had to try. Drin's concerned presence hovered beside him as he stepped forward with more certainty. The ground was solid beneath him. The precipice to his side seemed less of a concern. As he ascended the last incline on the balls of his feet, Katinka leaned from the arched doorway and grasped him by the shoulder.

"Hurry," she hissed. "Carly is coming by another path and will meet us at the top."

Thunder grumbled in the distance and the day grew darker. Drinia leapt from Katinka's shoulder, coasting on outstretched wings to latch onto Xeras's chest like an oversized broach. He cupped one hand protectively over her.

"His men may be close behind you and I saw Kassius

taking a path up the side of the mountain. Make haste." Katinka pushed him on ahead of her. "The anvil is at the top of the gate. I have prepared it according to the ritual of the closing. If you can make it work, I think we must hurry."

Thunder cracked again, harsh and close at hand, and a gust of wind swirled through the small alcove. A storm was descending fast. A short passage led directly up to the top surface of the great gate. There was no wall or balustrade. Dark, metallic clouds rolled down through a passage that cut deep between two mountains and he could glimpse snatches of the great high plains beyond.

The air sparked with ominous forces and unknown futures. The wind shrieked around him like a river of ice. Xeras sheltered in the scant cover of the door arch.

Ahead of him Carly stood, braced against the onslaught of nature, staring out into the keening darkness. All around them, low mists and high clouds mixed in confused skeins. Expectancy filled the air. Carly turned towards him, every line of his body drawn tense but ready. Xeras felt like a ghost in his own body, there but not there. Frozen by the certainty that all this would indeed be for naught. Out of the storm, a great form swooped down, so fast for its immense size.

He shouted against the wind, "Carly, get down, get down!"

But his voice was lost. Then a great armored hand snatched him—so quickly that it defied reason. The hand of a dragon, pallid like the first petals of a yellow flower, bearing him swiftly away.

Xeras just stood. His breath rasped in and out. The wind continued to howl, and Carly—was gone.

Chapter Fourteen

Katinka stood, her hair whipping in the wind, as she looked out after Ghardis, long gone from sight. Xeras raised his hand, trying to grasp reality itself and twist it into some acceptable shape. Into the mists, Carly and Ghardis had gone, beneath them the village crouched as nature began its onslaught with rain that hit in staccato waves. The storm drove down from the high plains scudding over the ground. And on that ground...

A dim shadow moved over the ground, not one cast by the passing clouds that blocked the sun. Xeras kept one hand clasped over Drinia trying to block the worst of the weather from her, but with the other he reached out and turned to Katinka. She resisted but glancing up at Xeras, he fixed his own gaze on the approaching line.

She saw then, and understood. They seemed small from this distance but there were so many. Plainsmen, streaming swiftly over the ground as if the winds of the storm drove them.

Fear squeezed Xeras's chest hard enough that he felt he could die on the spot. Katinka's eyes tightened as she comprehended what approached. She went back towards the alcove, apparently ready to either raise what defense she could or tell the citizens to flee while they had the chance.

He caught her arm with his free hand, still cradling Drinia awkwardly with the other. "The path is broken; there is no way through. Is there anywhere the people can go?"

As if in answer, a flurry of snow scudded over the exposed surface of the gate.

"Only into the hills," Katinka shouted. "Without shelter, or provisions beyond what they carry, with children and elders. They would be overtaken quickly but maybe the plainsmen would stop and not pursue once they took the town. And faint hope is better than none at all, unless you can close this gate." She waved to the alcove the path led to. A worn wooden handle pushed tight up against the wall. "But it is designed to respond only to the one who bears the chain of the office. It is the amulet to which the mechanism of the gate is meant to respond."

"I have an idea. I just need that damn Jarvice. Is there another way down?"

"Across the other side of the gate in about in the same place there is a second path. It emerges in one of the outbuildings." She grabbed his wrist where he held her and pulled him. In the open, the building storm drowned out his words as he called to her. "Katinka, Katinka wait..."

There is no time, Xeras. If she is to save any of her people she must act in haste.

Drin's voice came from inside, not competing with the whistling winds and roaring sky.

"She will hasten them to their doom," Xeras said quietly. But the one he needed to reach was Jarvice. And the dragon never responded to his spoken voice. Like Drin, Jarvice heard his feelings and his fears more than his words.

"Jarvice." He willed his need, his desire, his desperation at the stone dragon. And as if, and probably quite literally by, magic the creature's broad head appear over the edge of the bridge. Katinka faltered in her headlong charge as Jarvice blinked into the wind.

Xeras ordered his thoughts. He spoke softly, willing Jarvice to hear. "This is the realm, this Ballot's Keep to which your race and its very future is tied. And to preserve it I have two requests of you."

"It is not yet that realm. The bond is formed, to you from us, but not from you to them. You have days at best before our magics will poison you, unreleased. And that would make naught of all our plans."

"I need the duke. Who is the other dragon flying around up there?"

"It is Plegura."

"You have to get her to go after Ghardis."

"No one is swifter than Plegura, but Ghardis is stronger. She would not be able to stop him."

"Then she must take me after him. I must go where he goes. That is my first request."

Drin's voice was frail. *Is that what we have been waiting for? A chance for you to die by dragon and by falling at the same time. Something definitely unsurvivable.*

"Her mind is not given to holding any idea so complex for any great length of time. There would be a risk."

"So there would be a risk. If instead I am slain, there is no bond, there is no magic, there is no reason to hold Carly or to harm him—"

"There is no get. And the get is my only concern."

"And the duke is mine, and this town is his. And all these things must be together in harmony or all will perish. I must go after the duke and you must stay here and close the gate."

"The gate's magic is of a much earlier time before the era of Tirrin's empire. It is from an age when dragons were both more and less than now and people much the same, in their selfishness. The people who made this gate have guarded against their work being wrested from their control. To overcome their magics is beyond my powers."

"It is not," Xeras said firmly. "For with your wings outstretched, you can span the archway below us. And at rest, you are more impermeable even than solid stone. You can prevent anyone from coming through this gate until I return. You can seize this faint hope that the town will be saved, that I might return the duke to it and through my pledge bind your people to these people to begin a new dynasty, a new age, a new magic. It is still possible."

"It is a faint hope," the dragon said mildly.

"As a wisewoman just said to me, faint hope is better than no hope at all. You could keep me and Drinia here, but it will not be enough in the end to serve your needs, the needs of the dragon race. Reach for the greater prize, the slim hope, and we may yet have it all."

Xeras tried to send hope, to tear hope from his soul and throw it at Jarvice, the desperate need to find a solution to their peril. He felt somehow that Drin, silent for once, was doing the same. They could all still come through this, together.

Jarvice made no reply but Xeras could feel his skeptical assent. The dragon backed from the lip, several of the great stones dropped away in his wake and the whole structure of the gate trembled. Katinka pulled his arm impatiently, obviously frustrated by an exchange she couldn't hear and a dragon that seemed intent on destroying what was left of the great gate.

The path on the other side of the gate was roughly akin to the one he had come up. But with Katinka now in the lead they descended without any hint of caution. Katinka's skirts swirled behind her as she ran down a path gleaming with rain and sleet. Xeras grabbed the squirming Drinia, worried she might freeze to death before he could even begin to grapple with their many perils. He held her with both hands against his stomach as he pelted after Katinka knowing that if he slipped there would be nothing to grab onto.

He was winded and gasping by the time they got to the top of the stairs. Katinka paused a moment, as she grasped the heavy bar. They had no way of knowing if someone was on the other side of the door. Xeras skidded to a stop, Katinka reached out to steady him. Then together they wrenched up the bar. As she pulled open the door, Xeras was closer to the doorway. The stairway was dark and empty beyond.

"Go. Hurry," she urged.

Go carefully, Drin contradicted firmly. *As you said, all things together will make this work. Not only the duke and his people, the dragons and the get, but you also as the one thing that unites them. Breaking your neck on the stairs would doom this whole enterprise.*

The steep stairs were far more treacherous on the way down with nothing to stop anyone who fell from tumbling to the base. Katinka crowded behind him as they spilled out into a close, cold room.

"Fruit cellar," Katinka said tersely. She fumbled in the dark for the door.

She took a few steps into the open and faltered to a stop. Xeras stumbled into her, dropping Drinia who protested with a squeal and scampered away from his groping hand. By the look of her, the cold didn't bother her much. On his knees, he finally glanced up and saw what had stopped Katinka in her tracks.

It was only the roughest of estimations that had caused

Xeras to believe Jarvice could block the entrance of the gate. It proved to be barely the case. With his wings flared to their fullest extent, he spanned the void leaving a narrow gap into which Jarvice's neck fitted as he reared up. He gave Xeras one last marble-eyed look as if to suggest this was not quite how he had planned to spend his winter, and then with a shiver underwent his uncanny transformation. Within moments all that was left was a rock face with barely any features to suggest a sentient creature lay beneath.

"That's what you were talking to the dragon about," Katinka said.

Parlen ran up to her. "What is the creature doing! Is he trying to trap us in here?"

"The plainsmen are attacking," Katinka said, now quite steady. "Gather the council. I will stand in my brother's place. We must assume the plainsmen might move in small numbers through the narrow paths."

"Without their horses?" Parlen asked skeptically.

"They would not normally attack in force without sending messengers or spokespeople first to talk. We cannot assume anything about their actions now with the Tirrinian stirring things up. Speaking of which..."

Other people were coming out of the houses to peer up at the sealed gate.

Parlen's grizzled face creased with a scowl. "That Kassius made a tearful farewell to the princess and is saddling up with his men." He stopped, looked at Katinka. "Stand in your brother's place?"

"The dragon took him," Katinka explained. "The yellow one."

Parlen looked from her to Xeras, as if expecting some response. A shadow passed overhead. Parlen and Katinka shrank back against the wall as Plegura's lithe form passed overhead, low enough for her tail to glance off a chimneystack with a clatter. His second request.

He waited for Drin's protest but the ghost seemed, for once, resigned.

"Try and keep Kassius here," Xeras said. "If all goes well, you are going to need him, or people like him. The easiest manner will probably be to keep Phinia here, if he cares for her..."

"Why on earth—" Parlen began.

But Katinka hushed him. "What do you plan to do?"

"I plan to go after Carly."

"Would he still be alive?" Katinka asked plainly but with hope.

"The dragon came here, and that cannot be a coincidence. Somehow the conclave had Carly brought to them. Perhaps Ghardis, being the slower witted sort, still gave his allegiance to the last to honor the bond. Or maybe his will was malleable to the waning magics of the Tirrinian mages. But even in rash actions, the Tirrinian conclave is cautious. They might well leave Carly alive because it keeps more options open for them."

That was more a statement of his hopes than his beliefs. Despite his parentage, he had never been groomed for a seat in the conclave. He had no direct knowledge of their working. But he had heard his father hold forth on such matters often enough to have some notion.

He saw Plegura swoop down on the far side of the town and strode forward to meet her. Then remembering Drinia, he stopped and turned, pulling the pouch up from under his tunic. Drinia sat on the ground, giving him a cagey look.

"It is either this or be left behind," he told her.

With a huff she launched upwards. Flapping her wings twice, she scrambled onto his shoulders. Her first real flight.

Chapter Fifteen

Xeras came to some understanding of Drinia's perspective. Being carried by some enormous creature careening around in terrible weather was a fairly unpleasant proposition, especially if you weren't sure where said creature was going. Yet it still seemed to be only the late afternoon when a resounding jolt brought him out of a miserable fugue. Plegura dropped him rather abruptly onto a familiar stretch of paving stones, like a dog dropping a toy it has suddenly lost interest in.

A journey that had taken him months on foot was reversed in a few hours. He got shakily to his feet and looked around the walkway along the lee side of the main town of Tirrin. Plegura shuffled back and regarded him blankly. There was something of a crowd, also, compacted by having pressed themselves as far back from the dragon as they could.

"I don't suppose a dragon is like a penny-punt, and can be instructed simply to wait at my pleasure," Xeras said. "But on the whole you are the only arguable asset I have in doing..." Then remembering himself he continued in the dragon language. "Stay here, please. Wait for me."

Plegura, although attentive, showed no particular comprehension. Xeras smiled and nodded as he backed away, hoping she wouldn't forget she wasn't meant to eat him.

Well, despite the discomfort of the transit, he had been given some time to think. As much as he hated to admit it, the only person with any interest, albeit it one of blood more than amity, was his father. His father would probably know what Kassius had been sent to do.

It was a fairly brief walk from the coast, up one of the main streets of the town to his father's house in the wealthier district on the hill. He took it quickly before the townspeople got a chance to call the guard on him. Despite a lifetime in Tirrin, it all looked somehow new. The streets were clogged with laboring men and women dressed in the proscribed browns and greys. Servants had badges on their chests to mark their house. A few men of rank noticed his progress but no one stopped him as he made his way in all haste.

He saw Plegura rise up from the dockway with a tumultuous buffeting of her wings and winced as she circled and settled on the hooded peak of one of the lower towers, not without some cost to its stone and tilework.

Striding up the stairs, he swung open the great double doors, always left unlocked because the footmen and butler behind it were security enough. During the day, anyway, and in times of peace.

"My father is in?" Xeras made his way past the same elderly butler and two unfamiliar footmen. Assurance, indicative of class, was quite sufficient.

The fates were with him as he opened the door to his father's day suite and found the man himself in residence. He looked smaller. His richly embroidered clothes stiff and overextravagant. His face was blank, the only expression that suggested surprise in a man so calculating. One of his ubiquitous runners stood at his shoulder, a thin woman from a house high enough to wear clothing with fur and trim, albeit brown fur and trim. He waved for her to leave them alone.

"I am told you arrived on dragonback," he said with clear disdain.

Xeras was somewhat preoccupied by Drinia who was wiggling her way loose again. The get emerged from his tunic and climbed to perch on his shoulder. She flared her wings and made quite a new kind of sound, a vicious hiss that exposed rows of tiny but sharp-looking teeth.

"I was carried in more like a piece of baggage. It is the less dignified option, but marginally less apt to get one killed by an unfortunate fall."

Although if you keep trying, you will manage it eventually.

Speaking of untimely.

"You have destroyed generations of carefully laid plans." His father stood, his hands rather primly on his hips.

"It is, of course, the only purpose of my life to hamper plans of yours. I am somewhat handicapped by having not the faintest idea of what those plans might be!"

Xeras!

Xeras drew himself up, sucking in and holding his breath. A man died. This trivia of expectation and resentment meant nothing now. All that was important was that Carly not be added to the list of casualties.

"Father, I am here only because I need to know where the conclave had the duke of Ballot's Keep taken. I need to see him and I need him alive. Because if there is one thing worse than the conclave, it will be the conclave with a fresh input of dragon magic running amok across the mainland again. I know this might not—"

"I quite agree."

"What?" Xeras knew himself not to be the most reasonable

of men at the best of times, and after he had stood in that stinking cell next to Drin's emaciated body he could hardly bear to be in the same room as the man again. But this wasn't about him, it wasn't about Drin. "You agree that the high houses of Tirrin must not benefit from dragon magic."

"You must know my position on that, son. It is your goals that have changed."

His father was always so grudging in his emotion, dour and disapproving. Xeras wanted to understand just what the hell was going on here, but at the same time resisted being distracted even for a moment from his goal.

"I didn't know about any of this, father. You never told me a damn thing about it, nor did I want to know. But whatever the reason, if you can tell me where the duke is, do it now."

Harus stood stiffly before him. Light streamed down on him from the open windows overhead. He seemed uncharacteristically hesitant.

"If a big yellow dragon has landed somewhere in this town and left a man here, then someone noticed it. And if someone noticed it, then someone told you about it. At least tell me if this has happened."

He fought the urge to reach out and shake his father as if the information could be jarred loose.

"Yes," Harus said. "This has happened. And I know the dragon brought the duke here. It's the work of a faction devoted to returning Tirrin to the great power and influence it once knew, and now they will be looking for you. For the duke interests them very little. He was only the means to securing the one thing really needed. I know that person is you, and given the nature of your own arrival they must know it too. We are not safe here. I sent Circia to arrange a punt to collect us from the water door."

"I am not going down into the dark canals with you without some explanation."

"And I cannot tell you where I plan to take you, until I have reason to trust you. Son..."

Harus stepped towards him, arm outstretched, as if to grasp him by the shoulder. Xeras froze, unsure how to react. The sight of this man caused only revulsion. He had barely touched Xeras in all the years he could remember. Yet in trying to win Carly back from Tirrin, his father was the only one to whom Xeras could turn. If he had, in some small way, to play the part of a dutiful son in order to accomplish his ends...

Drinia had no such compunction. With another hiss she launched herself at Harus with a flurry of wing beats. Harus flinched and swatted at her, flinging the dragonling away against the wall. Xeras stooped to grab her as she crouched to launch another attack.

"Drinia, hold," he said sternly. She seemed entirely uninjured and growled with undeterred aggression.

"Drinia?" Harus said with disgust, his hand going to his scalp where a serious of shallow scratches oozed. "You know that the names of the destroyed are never to be spoken again."

"Drinia," Xeras repeated. "If I have any goals, Father, they formed only on the day Drin died. I mean for his death to haunt this place. I mean for it to haunt you for as long as I draw breath and beyond. As he haunts me."

Xeras, Xeras, I have tried so hard to explain. I am not here to punish you. Can you truly not understand?

Harus dabbed at his head with the end of his sleeve. "We cannot tarry, Xeras. But I do understand."

"You understand? How could you possibly understand?"

Harus took a deep breath, looking nervously to the main

door. He went to a panel in the corner, a disguised door Xeras was not meant to know about and Harus apparently hesitated to expose even now.

He pulled open the panel. "You must have heard the tale by now, about your mother."

Pressing his fingers to his brow, Xeras felt the squeezing pressure build inside him. His mother, he was told, had died in childbirth. Just the first and most comprehensive example of the destructive effect he had on the lives of others. His father never spoke of her.

Nor even let you know her name. Xeras, did you truly never guess? Never hear a whisper?

That was a resounding, shuddering crash from outside the room, in the lobby. Voices raised and a cascade of footfalls. Events were overtaking him again. Xeras preceded his father into the hidden stairway; it smelt of damp and must. The passageway sloped sharply down the house's waterdoor, opening onto the canal that passed beneath. It was not so much a door as a metal grill flat on the floor and barred from the inside. Lifting it, Xeras saw the runner Harus had been speaking to before. She held a bar near the door, using her feet to position a small punt beneath it. On the seat of the punt, a guttering lantern cast the only light.

It was dark all around. They were in the city's canals, which had become little more than blackwater sewers as the buildings closed over them. Xeras was hampered by his long tunic, ample fabric intended for a somewhat broader man, and he grew concerned with Drinia who scrabbled and flapped at his shoulder apparently intent on keeping his father in sight. He dropped gracelessly into the vessel without upsetting its balance. His father followed, rather more adeptly despite his portly frame—more practiced, no doubt.

"And who, exactly, would tell me such a tale, Father? Your staff would not. Your enemies had little interest in me because *I* had no interest in the insular politics of this place and so was not of use to them. If it is something you want to tell me, tell me. I'll not beg for your indulgences. That is not why I am here."

Circia stood at the back of the punt, leaving them just enough room to sit facing each other, seated on planks across the slender vessel.

"Your lack of interest in my wishes has always been quite clear," Harus muttered. "I never wanted you to beg or fawn upon me. But if you had the slightest interest in your mother you might, just once, have asked."

"When I was young, I asked. I asked my nurse, my nanny, the butler. I asked the people who were *there* to be asked and they would not tell me. They would not tell me, because you did not want me to know. I accepted that. I accepted all the limitations you placed on what I was to do, and not do, to know and not know, to be and not be. I was not a good son to you, but I tried to be a tolerable one until the last. Until you killed the one man I did love. And there is no going back from that. So tell me anything it pleases you to tell me, but do not expect me to care."

And what angered him most of all was how easily he slipped into being so desperate not to care. He had assumed that Drin's death had been a threshold, a severing of all ties to his muddy and unilluminating past with all its self-involved secrets and lies. He had met people living straightforward, well-meaning lives. He had seen his own character cast in sharp relief, and it was the character of Tirrin, so invested in being important, at any cost. Xeras made an effort, an immense effort, to just let it all go, to genuinely not care, not need, not cling to all of this which had been his world. He felt himself relax.

His father was silent, as usual.

"Do you know where the duke is?" Xeras asked plainly. "That, now, is all I need to know."

"What you do will affect the lives of thousands, you need to understand—"

"I don't, Father. That is your way. I care for Carly, Duke of Ballot's Keep. He is my friend, and he is threatened, and I am going to do all I can to see him safe. If you can take me to him, do so. Your reasons do not concern me."

Circia was taking them somewhere, that much was clear. Harus's silence stretched a while longer, then he spoke.

"I was very young when I met your mother. She was from a family very much on the cusp of high house status. Yulia..." he barely whispered the name. "She believed she was of the blood, and so of course I believed it too. When she fell pregnant, my own father made a more careful accounting. She fell short by just one degree. Yulia was not high house, although you, as her son and mine, were acceptable. The laws still applied. After she gave birth, they took her away and there was nothing I could do. She was convicted of miscegenation and her ignorance of her own true status was not accepted as a defense. I never knew exactly when she died or where her family buried her. I could do nothing. My own parent did not accept the child. It was greatly contested whether a child could count as being high-blooded if his mother was not. Without my protection, you would almost certainly have been killed. Do not think for a moment I did not love her, and mourn her. In a way it is hard to accept, even after all those years, that she is gone. That is why I took you to see Drin. As terrible as that sight was for you, I knew it was better than to never see it with your own eyes and to never truly know he was gone."

He spoke softly, almost dispassionately. His words echoed

faintly of the confusion of arches and columns as the punt drifted on the placid waters under the city. The space was too tight to use the pole which lay along the punt's side. Circia simply guided them with her hands on the bricks and stones and, in some places, bars or ropes were strung to aid passage.

Xeras said nothing. He had nothing to say. Drinia pressed in against his neck, her wings folded tightly back. Perhaps he was meant to offer some kind of comfort to a man who had let his lover be taken to that worst of fates. Should he be grateful his father had decided to save him? Did he believe that? It sounded rather like a post-hoc excuse for a man preserving not only his own life, but his wealth and status also.

It was all beside the point. "The duke," he prompted.

"Shortly after I lost Yulia," Harus continued implacably. "I was approached by a faction of the conclave who sat in opposition to the dominant clique of which my father was a member. Given the raw power, both political and magical, that they faced, they acted cautiously and in utter secrecy. Their goal being to break down the division between the high houses and the other houses of Tirrin. They were aware that many times over the great expanse of human history, the dragons have forged alliances with certain groups and given them power."

"This I know, father."

Harus scowled, but was not to be hurried. "But the connection is eventually severed and the magic fades. It can be preserved by breeding true. Thus in Tirrin, it was a single family that grew and divided many times during the period of the bond. Six generation before our current living memory, the dragon withdrew from us, the territories collapsed but for our few estates on the mainland. The many families could never again go back to being one. Those who still held a little magic began to be seen not as the last of our strength, but as a threat and so ironically it was they who began this movement. Our goal was to return Tirrin to its true nature, to this island where the soul of our people is succored. We began by means of many subtle spells to cause all memory of the dragon's power, the price, their very existence to fade away. And it was working..."

Xeras glanced up at Circia who stared ahead as she navigated the punt, feigning indifference. Or perhaps, as intuition suggested, none of this was news to her. Despite his apparent solitude his father must have had some confidants, some intimates.

He understood what his father was saying. But doubted it. There were always opposing interests playing across the high houses. Expansionists looked back to the golden age of the empire, homelanders looked back even further to a time when Tirrin culture arose on the island with a complex interaction of seafarers, farmers and exiles. They saw the great expansion as a poisoning of that culture that resulted in the infamous abuses, exploitation and the bloody wars that followed.

Taking a deep breath Xeras tried to think of how to insert his own immediate needs into the morass of old history and new disclosures.

You can take Carly and the dragons of this precious island for good. Leave the old bastard to his schemes.

"I must ask," Harus said. "You say you had no goals. But it cannot be sheer happenstance that you somehow got hold of documents we had worked so hard and so carefully to suppress, taken up even the study of their language, and now this..."

He gestured to Drinia with a flick of his hand as if he might be contaminated just by pointing in her direction.

"Perhaps someone else put the books in my path, but I

studied them solely because it irritated you," Xeras said. "That was really pretty much the only goal at that time. But if I understand that you want dragons and everyone related to them out of Tirrin, we have discovered one thing we have in common albeit for different reasons. Now why is it we are heading deep under the city, because I am close to deciding I would be better off jumping out and wading for daylight."

Circia glanced down. One thing she seemed to have in common with his father was the ability to communicate a great depth of disdain without saying a single word. It probably helped that they were nearing the centre of the town now and the water below them was way over his head in depth. An apt metaphor, perhaps.

"The one place I cannot easily enter is the dungeons," Harus said. "If it is so crucial to see how your duke is faring, I do have the right to place any person under arrest. I can have you put in with him, but it will not take long for news of your presence to spread."

"I need only a few moments. If I had been more timely, it would not have required such lengths."

Circia brought them deftly through the narrow passageways and finally out into a steep alleyway that led up the courtyard before the council building below which the thick-walled cells crouched in their total darkness. These were places people could be stored away for as long as required, or disposed of without anyone hearing a sound.

"I should not be doing this," his father said. "The best that can be hoped for is that I am delivering you to the dragons whose influence must be entirely evil. It is far more likely that, like your mother before you, I am abandoning you to your death. But despite anything you might think, you are my son and I will always try to aid you."

The light shone down in a yellow shaft from above, striking across the boat so Harus and Circia both squinted up at Xeras as he stood carefully to step onto the old stone stair worn into sagging, bowed shapes by the passage of thousands of feet.

Above him, where the stairs broke into the courtyard, two liveried guardsmen stood. Xeras realized that Harus must have taken a somewhat circuitous path to this place, to leave time for the guards to be in place.

This would have to count as a poorly thought-out plan, even compared to your previous efforts...

"You have, of course, put it about that you are turning me in, just as the majority of the conclave would require," Xeras said. "And I have no way to know if that is indeed what you are doing. And everything else is just another example of your consummate ability to manipulate."

Harus blinked at him. "If my powers were so great, you, of all people, would not doubt me."

Xeras kept his back to the guardsmen and bundled the disgruntled Drinia back into her hiding place. His final hope was, after all, parental duty and concern.

He had no parting words and offered none. Just fixed in his memory the picture of his father sitting in the darkness. Circia's hand rested subtly upon his shoulder. Xeras turned and walked up the stairs.

CB

If the guardsmen merely acted a part at his father's behest, they did so with some vigor. He was propelled into the dark cell, falling on his hands and knees on the fouled floor. He didn't want to know, really. In this moment it could all still be all right but if he called and found—

"Xeras, is that you?"

Carly's voice. And with it, Carly's hand that, fumbling in the darkness, found the side of his head, his ear, his cheek.

"Oh, no," Carly said. "It *is* you."

He helped Xeras to his feet. It was totally dark. He could not detect as much as a single chink or speck of light.

"There is something I need to say to you, Carly."

"And what is that?"

"I rather hope you don't require any particular ceremony with props and witnesses for this. I want to pledge to you, Carly Duke of Ballot's Keep, my loyalty, my allegiance and my obedience for so long as I live."

"Your obedience I will not require," Carly replied. "But your loyalty and allegiance I accept, gladly. I duly declare you a citizen in full standing of the township of Ballot's Keep. Now was there—"

The room cracked, the air flashed. A faint luminescence endured with a subtle blueish glow. It washed over and into Xeras, through him and beyond.

"A lot of people will have noticed that." Xeras drew out the pouch and Drinia emerged with a discontented sneeze. "This is the reason, you understand, that I couldn't...before when you approached me I would want you to think. You know, this is a good time to..."

Babble like an idiot?

"Quite," Xeras concluded.

"There is more to whatever you are planning, I hope." Carly moved to the door. He wedged his foot against it.

"Barely." Xeras held Drinia in his hands and she, for once was cooperative. "Drinia, my dear, we need to call your mother."

Drinia looked up at him placidly. "I appreciate you might not have the widest possible perspective on this but we are, once again, in a situation where one or both of us will shortly be deceased without some...blast."

Drinia quite clearly wasn't going to be very much help.

"I am being quite patient," Carly said. "But perhaps you would care to explain."

Xeras reached out, resting his hand on Carly's chest. "Given our circumstances, you are altogether too understanding, and too patient. And these are not things I had previously thought could be faults. But if they are, they are character flaws entirely necessary in anyone who would put up with me, even in the capacity of follower."

"You have proven your capacity to follow me wherever I go, but..."

"We need Plegura. She is our only way out of here, and it is quite possible she will bring the building down on us and kill us before getting us out if she responds at all."

Xeras took a deep breath and tried to push aside the wash of reassurance he felt just at being with Carly, no matter what the circumstances. "Plegura," he called, trying to direct his will outward. "Plegura, we need you. Plegura, your get needs you. Plegura, Plegura."

And as he watched, the small glowing motes in the air eddied like seeds in the winds and streamed out through the walls.

"Plegura, we need you. Plegura, we need out of here."

The small lights kept streaming outwards, emerging from his own body. As he redoubled his efforts, they glowed brighter and moved faster, swirling and piercing beyond the walls of the cell as if they did not even exist.

Plegura, however, did not seem in a great hurry to arrive and Xeras began to feel...tired. There was a clank at the door and Carly threw himself against it trying to hold it shut. Muffled shouting and calls came through the door as it shook with ever greater reverberations. Xeras was frightened now, truly frightened.

"Plegura!"

And the building resounded with a much louder crash. Dust and dirt cascaded down from the ceiling. Xeras stumbled forward, next to Carly in the hope the interior wall might protect them.

"Carefully, Plegura. Carefully!"

You might have mentioned that a little earlier. I don't think she is listening now.

The ceiling dropped great heavy stones and light broke through. Plegura's paws clawed through and reached forward. Xeras grabbed Drinia with one hand and with the other reached out to Carly.

"Hold onto me," he shouted over the general carnage.

Carly scooped own arm around Xeras's waist as Plegura grasped them both, yanking them out of the building roughly. A stone dropping from the gaping masonry struck him hard on the temple and his senses dissolved into a confusion of light, wind and motion. Drinia peeped and Carly cursed, holding so tight onto him that it was hard to breathe.

CB

The passage of time became a little vague. Plegura had them. He tried to think of Ballot's Keep but couldn't collect his thoughts.

Think about being put down now. It has obviously become your life's purpose to get killed by a dragon one day, but today does not have to be that day.

But Xeras just thought of Ballot's Keep. Him and Drinia and the duke and the people of Ballot's Keep and, Gods help them all, the magic and the plainsmen. But mostly of Ballot's Keep.

But maybe Drin's insidious voice caused his mind to wander, because he felt the dragon's hold on his body loosen and the all too familiar sensation of falling. He had one surprisingly calm thought. He and Carly and Drin, together, in whatever place people go to. It didn't seem so bad.

Then a confusion of tumbling, wet coldness, over and over. Then stillness. Nothing but a faint crackling sound and the susurration of the wind. Xeras put it together rather slowly. He lay face down in snow, his legs pointing uphill. A tentative peep rather suggested that Drinia had made it through okay.

"Xeras," Carly called out.

Somewhat reluctantly he rolled over and inspected himself, soiled, rumpled, yet apparently whole.

Carly waded towards him. "That dragon dropped us." He rivaled Drin in his capacity to state the obvious.

"Yes, well apparently she suffers from a short attention span," Xeras said faintly. "Do you have any idea where we are?"

Carly knelt by him. Snow fell thickly all around. "We have rock, snow and trees. It could be almost anywhere. But I have a feeling it is somewhere in the mountain duchies, if only I can get my bearings." He pulled Xeras under the partial shelter of some stunted trees. "It will do no one any good if we freeze to death after all this."

Xeras laughed. Somehow it would be all too fitting. He had stumbled onto success in all the ways that mattered. The bond was formed, Carly was alive, the gate was, after a fashion, closed. But they might still freeze to death on a mountainside.

Drinia scrambled up his boot in her usual presumptuous manner, clawing and peeping for attention.

"You stay here," Carly said. "Take my cloak. I will climb a little higher and get some idea of where we are."

"*You* stay here," Xeras replied. "I've come too far to lose you in the snow storm."

"Maybe I should have specified obedience after all." Carly pushed the cloak at him and forged up through the thick snow.

℣

It took several days to make their way back through the congested passes to Ballot's Keep. It was a cold, tough proposition and Xeras should have been miserable. But he wasn't.

Drinia truly did seem immune to the cold. She flew awkwardly, clambered and gamboled, as if the whole excursion were arranged just for her entertainment. They walked together. Carly's hand around Xeras's shoulder. They lay together at night in whatever shelter they could find. They were too hard pressed for any hint of passion, but to feel Carly's arms around him was to feel complete.

Finally, near dusk on the third day they stumbled out of the trees to see Kassius mounted on the back of a very morose-looking Thurstian horse. "Finally," Kassius said impatiently. "My scrying is getting weaker every day, but the rest of the town is positively abuzz with new and unpredictable talents."

Carly stood forward, shielding Xeras. "What is it exactly that you plan to do?"

"Oh, no need to bristle my lord Duke. Tirrin has recognized Ballot's Keep. They felt it wise once Xeras was gone, leaving in his wake a few demolished buildings. And I am their ambassador, at least until the thaw. Which is just as well as you now have dozens of people evincing magical skills and not a single one of them well versed in how to use them safely, but for me." Kassius dismounted. "Phinia and I are planning a spring wedding and there is clearly a case to be made for defection if my posting here is not made permanent. But I dare say it won't come to that. Tirrin, above all things, likes to be well informed."

Kassius indicated that they looked in more need of a steed than he. Katinka appeared, riding in the track Kassius had forged. She called out, "Brother, dear. This is truly the last time I allow you to go off adventuring without me."

"Xeras, take the horse," Carly said vaguely as he waited for her to meet them.

"If I were a prouder man, I would argue that I can manage," Xeras replied. "But seeing as you suggested that obedience was desirable, if not mandatory..."

Carly was not really listening. He went to Katinka, leaving Kassius to help Xeras to mount the fidgeting horse, rather a different sort from the late lamented Lefty.

It was hard to imagine this was it. He was going home with his duke, his lover, to his town to a real life. Sure there was still the matter of the gate and whatever Kassius had done to sow discord with the plainsmen, but somehow this future was too golden to quite be believable.

"How far are we from the town?" Xeras asked with a parched voice.

"Not far." Kassius pointed up between the branches.

Xeras glimpsed a curl of pale smoke barely visible against the indigo sky. The Gods alone knew what really awaited him in

Ballot's Keep. Somehow it seemed as if the townsfolk would eventually repudiate any camaraderie they offered. He had no way to know if he was capable of being the kind of man this kind of place needed.

But you are curious, darkling. It was always your problem, eh? Why don't you go see?

Xeras looked down at Kassius who led his horse for him, apparently content to go afoot while Carly swung up behind his sister on her mount. They went on to lead the way.

Kassius met Xeras's eyes, his expression unreadable. "The party of plains dwellers who aspire to possessing more arable land and a more settled way of life, they—"

"Kassius, why are you telling me this?"

"That, my surly countryman, will become clear if you shut up and listen. I am not thrilled with requiring your help, but the fact of the matter is thus. I provoked a faction who harbored dormant desires to seize the town. Women for the most part, as fearsome as warriors as their men. There was one who needed only a little encouragement to rise as a leader and draw the others to her. And once begun, her band is fixed on their goal of invasion."

And...?

"And..."

Kassius glanced around, making sure they were not overheard. "And her name is Yulia."

About the Author

To learn more about Emily Veinglory, please visit www.veinglory.com. Send an email to Emily Veinglory at veinglory@gmail.com or join her Yahoo! group to join in the fun with other readers http://groups.yahoo.com/group/veinglory.

Would you sell your soul for the find of a lifetime?
Could you give up your life for love?

Revenant
© *2007 Olivia Lorenz*

On Santorini, vampires are more than folklore—and the workers on Jack Hunter's archaeological dig know the body he's found is meant to stay buried.

But Jack isn't one for superstition. Despite the warnings, he takes the skeleton to his house for safekeeping. There, he finds a mysterious letter from a man named Belas, offering directions to a site of great importance in return for a small favour: his blood.

Belas is a vrykolakas, the most feared and dangerous of all Greek vampires. Millennia ago, the island's high priest sacrificed his family to calm the rage of the volcano. Belas committed suicide to ensure that his spirit would remain restless, thereby cursing the high priest to suffer a similar fate. But the priest escaped to Crete, and as a vampire cannot cross salt water, Belas has been waiting four thousand years to exact his vengeance. Now he intends Jack to be the agent of his revenge.

Available now in ebook and print from Samhain Publishing.

Enjoy the following excerpt from Revenant...

At the back of the church stood a few wooden chairs Jack guessed must belong to the older members of the community. Whenever he had attended an Orthodox service, he had found the congregation to stand or sit upon the floor as the rites decreed. To someone raised to view the busy pews of Anglicanism as the norm, it still disconcerted Jack to see so much empty space in a church.

He moved towards the altar, which was draped with purple cloth for Lent. A wooden crucifix stood upon it, flanked by two creamy beeswax candles. Jack closed his eyes and inhaled, hoping for the scent of the candles, but all he could smell was a fusty trace of incense. Still, it calmed him. He opened his eyes again and looked up at the sunlight filtering through the tiny, thick glass windows to strike the crucifix.

Jack was half-admiring the simple play of light and shadow when Belas spoke behind him.

"Sacrifice," he said. "I have yet to learn of a religion that does not demand it."

Jack did not dare to turn around. "You're in a church."

"As you say. Why, Yianni, are you of the opinion that I should not be here?"

"If you were what you claim to be, then theologically speaking you should be unable to walk on consecrated ground," Jack said. "But I admit I am more than a little confused as to what you really are."

Belas's laughter rounded up into the dome. "I have claimed nothing for myself. You alone have decided that I am—what, precisely? A demon? Satan's imp?"

Jack felt foolish. "You want blood. To me that suggests vampirism."

"Certainly I am a predator," Belas purred, his breath hot and sudden against the back of Jack's neck. "And what predator does not relish the taste of blood?"

Jack turned his head, enough to glimpse a flash of copper-streaked hair, enough to feel the press of Belas's cheek against his neck. "I fear you find me poor game, if you see yourself as a hunter."

"Not at all," Belas replied, cheerful. "You constantly surprise me. I can think of no other creature I've encountered that came so willingly, and then behaved with such contradiction. How many times have I told you not to look at me? And yet you keep trying."

Jack jerked his head to stare fixedly at the altar in front of him. As an admission of guilt it was unmistakable and Belas laughed again.

"Oh, it's not just that. Did I not direct you to Akrotırı, where great treasures lie beneath the ash? And yet you insist on grubbing around in that horrid little shrine."

The mention of the shrine made Jack want to turn. "What do you know of that?"

"Enough." Belas's voice slid against him. "But I did not come here to discuss it."

"No?"

"Your innocence will be my downfall," Belas said. His hand rubbed through Jack's hair, starting at the nape of his neck and ruffling upwards. It was too strong a touch to tickle, and yet Jack shivered in involuntary response.

"I have things to ask you," he said. "About Akrotiri. And about the shrine."

Belas made an impatient sound. "Later. Now is the time for more pleasurable pursuits. On your knees, Yianni, and let us pray together."

"Pray?" Jack repeated even as he sank down before the altar.

Belas's laugh wrapped around him. "Yes. We will pray. An activity that requires thought and words, contemplation and repose. So close your eyes, and we will begin."

Jack obeyed, even clasping his hands together before him. He tried to summon the opening words to the Lord's Prayer, but found himself too aware of the presence behind him.

Belas's hair tickled his face and neck. Belas's scent was heat and dust and darkness. Jack liked the way that Belas knelt behind him. It felt both protective and possessive. And he liked most of all the slow, nuzzled licks Belas gave him along the side of his neck and into the vulnerable hollow of his jaw.

"Pray for pleasure," Belas said against his skin, "and I promise I will give it."

GET IT NOW

GREAT cheap FUN

Discover eBooks!

THE FASTEST WAY TO GET THE HOTTEST NAMES

Get your favorite authors on your favorite reader, long before they're
out in print! Ebooks from Samhain go wherever you go, and work with
whatever you carry—Palm, PDF, Mobi, and more.

samhain
publishing
Ltd

WWW.SAMHAINPUBLISHING.COM